HISTOR

Chandragupta Maurya and the Greek Onslaught

Shruti Garodia is an incurable reader and writer, with an abiding passion for history. She loves bringing alive the past for children through storytelling. She is the co-author of *The History of India for Children* (Hachette India, 2018), a bestselling two-volume set. Shruti graduated from Cornell University, USA, and holds degrees in engineering and finance. She has lived in New York and London during her career in banking. A keen traveller, she loves to explore historic sites and museums, and enjoys trying new adventures like scuba diving, trekking, skiing and sailing.

Archana Garodia Gupta is the co-author of the bestselling *The History of India for Children*, and the author of *The Women Who Ruled India* (Hachette India, 2019). With a lifelong passion for books, languages, travel and history, she has a knack for weaving delightful nuggets of information into engaging tales. A leading national quizzer, she has won the 'Champion of Champions' title from BBC's *Mastermind India* and is regularly seen on national TV as an expert on the immensely popular *Kaun Banega Crorepati*. She was the national president of FICCI Ladies Organization. She holds an MBA from IIM-Ahmedabad and is the founder of Touchstone, a digital-first jewellery brand.

HISTORY HUNTERS

Chandragupta Maurya and the Greek Onslaught

Shruti Garodia
Archana Garodia Gupta

Illustrations by Priya Kuriyan

First published in 2022 by Hachette India
(Registered name: Hachette Book Publishing India Pvt. Ltd)
An Hachette UK company
www.hachetteindia.com

3

ISBN 978-93-91028-92-3

Hachette Book Publishing India Pvt. Ltd
4th & 5th Floors, Corporate Centre
Plot No. 94, Sector 44, Gurugram – 122003, India

Typeset by Manmohan Kumar, Delhi

Printed and bound in India
by Manipal Technologies Limited, Manipal

MEET THE

ZOYA ALI (12 years): A book-lover with a passion for learning about anything and everything…and sharing her knowledge, whether her friends want it or not. Her natural indolence is often overcome by her insatiable curiosity, which leads her into adventures.

EKNOOR SINGH (12 years): Zoya's outspoken best friend and comrade in arms. This fearless warrior is always willing to take on anyone, anytime, and is invariably the first to rush into the unknown.

ANSH DESAI (11 years): The youngest of the group, who is usually dragged reluctantly into various escapades. This loyal youngster is always on the lookout for tasty treats as a reaction to his mother's many health fads.

ROHAN MATHAI (13 years): A nature lover with an uncanny ability to make even wild animals trust him. This quiet, level headed teenager can always be counted upon.

ELFU (13 years): a mischievous young elephant who believes he's human – especially when it comes to food. Rohan's constant companion since childhood, Elfu depends on his 'big brother' to protect him, undeterred by their size difference.

It started pouring suddenly on the way home. Though their school was just a few minutes away, the three children were drenched within seconds as they plodded along on a road that was rapidly turning to mud.

Eknoor started jumping along, splashing in all the puddles she saw.

Looking up from the book she had been trying to read while walking, Zoya said crossly, 'Would you stop that! You're getting my book all wet.'

Unfortunately, just then, a car with a trailer attached to it barrelled by, splattering muddy water all over them.

'What the...' spluttered Zoya. The new book she had borrowed from the library would be unreadable soon.

Ansh looked morose, but then that was his usual expression. 'Why is it raining in April in Goa?' he asked the universe glumly.

As the trio turned the corner, they saw the car entering the Miracle in the Forest Eco-Resort.

'Hey, is that the new wildlife expert?' said Eknoor, bouncing even more. 'Mummy said he was coming today. Apparently, he is driving up from Kerala with a full zoo!

She heard that this uncle can speak to animals! I wonder if there will be a tiger... And – '

'What nonsense!' broke in Ansh. 'Where on earth would they put a tiger in the resort...is he going to sleep in your room? Anyway, I heard a boy is coming with him too. I'll be so happy to have another boy around...Maybe he plays cricket!'

'Girls can play cricket too,' chorused Zoya and Eknoor in bored tones. This was an old argument.

• • • • • • • • • • • • • •

As they reached the gates of the resort, they heard a commotion. Zoya's and Eknoor's parents were speaking to a distinguished-looking man with grey hair. Standing next to him was a tall teenage boy.

'Welcome, Mr Mathai,' said Zoya's father, 'I am Riaz Ali, the general manager, and this is my wife, Farah. We are so excited to have you here at last!'

Eknoor's father, the head chef, chimed in. 'Hello, *ji*! Myself Harpreet Singh. This is my missus. You must be hungry after such a long drive. Please come and have chai and pakoras.'

As soon as he said this, there was a harrumphing noise. A long trunk daintily poked out of the wooden trailer, sniffing the air hopefully before prodding the tall boy's shoulder.

The boy didn't even look up as he said, 'Hush, Elfu! You're not getting any pakoras today. You've got to learn to like elephant food.'

There was astonished silence.

'Err...is that an elephant in there?' Ansh said incredulously. 'Does it understand English?'

The boy looked up at the three younger kids and gave a small grin. 'Elfu here truly understands the language of food. He has been hungry for as long as I've known him... which is our whole lives!'

'Can we meet him?' asked Eknoor excitedly.

Her mother immediately said a little nervously, 'First, let's see if it's safe, *beta*. Elephants are so awfully big...'

Mr Mathai said, 'Don't worry, Mrs Singh. Elfu is totally tame and gentle. I hand-reared him alongside Rohan – he is like a second son to me.'

'You mean your third son, Dad,' said the tall boy with a chuckle. 'Bhai won't be happy to hear about how you keep blanking him out.'

'Oh, yes!' Mr Mathai said with an embarrassed smile. 'My elder son has been away in the US for so long.'

Again, there was an impatient harrumph. Rohan went and opened the gate of the trailer. A curious trunk emerged, followed by a grey, leathery head and body, swaying along gracefully in the peculiar way that elephants do. Elfu stopped next to Rohan, looking about here and there, his trunk draping companionably along the boy's neck.

Zoya asked, 'Is Elfu a baby? He seems rather short for a full-grown elephant. He's barely a few inches taller than you, Rohan.'

'Oh no, he is all of thirteen years,' Rohan said, 'but just a bit small for his age – aren't you, Elfu?'

Eknoor walked close to Elfu's trunk and exclaimed, 'What is this beautiful mark on his forehead? It looks just like a bindi!'

Everyone turned to look at Elfu's forehead. Not only did he have the small pink spots common in Asian elephants, but he also had a perfect pink five-pointed star-shaped mark right in the middle of his forehead that looked for all the world like it had been painted on!

'Yeah, so we call Elfu the star of the family!' Mr Mathai's laughter boomed out at his lame joke, and Rohan rolled his eyes.

As the children trooped behind the adults towards the staff canteen, they started chatting with the new boy.

Zoya said, 'Ooh, I do love Happy Uncle's delish pakoras. By the way, I'm Zoya. Twelve. Mr Riaz Ali is my father. We helped set up Miracle in the Forest right from the start, two years ago. I've lived here in Goa ever since.'

Eknoor said, 'Noor. Twelve. My father is the chef here. I just love adventures, and I'm not scared of anything!'

Ansh gave her a withering look and said, 'I'm eleven. Ansh Desai. I moved here from Mumbai with my mum a few months ago.'

The new boy grinned. 'Hi, I'm Rohan Thomas Mathai. I'm thirteen, so the oldest here.' He gave a lopsided smile. 'I was quite unhappy to leave my home in Kerala, but this looks like it could be fun after all!'

He could never have imagined what lay ahead.

• • • • • • • • • • • • •

2

Zoya woke up the next morning with a big smile. The weekend was here, and her mom would be away meeting craftspeople in the nearby villages to buy items for her gift shop at the resort. There was no one to stop her from reading in bed all day. But just as she was about to turn over for another lazy snooze, a loud, piercing voice blasted through the window: 'Z-o-o-y-y-a-a, are you up? Let's go-o-o! We are taking Elfu on a picnic!'

'Argh,' Zoya groaned, flinging a hand across her eyes. She knew from experience that there was no way she was getting out of this. When her best friend was on a mission, nothing and no one could stop her.

Eknoor came in, bouncing with excitement as usual. She caught the look on Zoya's face and grinned. 'So…what were you planning to read today?' she asked.

'Well…the third book in the Fantastoria series is out and it was finally my turn to borrow it! I can't wait until Taria shows the intergalactic fleet she's boss…' trailed off Zoya.

'How can you choose to spend hours with your nose in a book?' said Eknoor, barely concealing a yawn. She could not understand Zoya's obsession with reading.

'Better than going around pretending to be some sort of James Bond all day,' flashed Zoya.

'JANE Bond, you mean!' chortled Eknoor, flexing her biceps. 'Okay, okay, just kidding! Now, get ready, and let's go.'

• • • • • • • • • • • • •

When they reached the garden in front of the staff houses, they spotted Ansh walking towards them, looking rather disgusted. He was holding a brown paper bag gingerly away from himself. 'Ma's contribution to our outing,' he explained briefly. 'She insists it's super healthy. You guys had better help me eat it.'

'Oh nooooo,' groaned the two girls. 'What is it today?' they asked nervously.

He wrinkled his nose. 'Umm, I guess some sugar-free, spice-free, oil-free, preservative-free…and absolutely taste-free nonsense.'

Ansh's mother was the in-house yoga-wellness-detox-spiritual expert for the resort. She was always offering up the strangest solutions and foods for every known – and unknown – ailment in the world, always with utmost faith and sincerity. Ansh found himself reluctantly gulping down concoctions in varying shades of green and brown all too frequently.

'Hey, maybe that pet elephant will eat it,' said Ansh, his eyes brightening at the thought.

'He has a name!' said Eknoor fiercely. 'How would you like it if I started calling you "that small human"? Animals are people too, you know…' she stopped when she saw the knowing glint in the eyes of the other two.

Ansh and Zoya looked at each other and chimed, 'Ignore-Kaur! She's-at-it-once-more!' It was another matter that mostly everybody called her Noor. And that's how she usually introduced herself too.

Noor glared at them and said, 'It's Eknoor. Not Ignore! I was going to say that Pops has offered to make a picnic basket for all of us, but I guess I'll tell him to make it just for one. Humph!' As head chef, feeding everybody he met seemed to be Harpreet Singh's mission in life.

Meanwhile, Rohan had joined them. 'Where should we go for our picnic?' he asked. 'It can't be around too many people as they invariably want to play with Elfu, and it takes ages to get anywhere with this brute.' He glared affectionately at the elephant behind him.

Wiggling his eyebrows knowingly, Ansh said, 'I know the perfect place! Girls, let's take them to – '

'Yay! Awesome idea! Wear your swimsuits, everyone!' squealed Noor and ran off.

As the kids returned, Mr Singh came up with a big basket from which all sorts of delicious smells were emanating. 'Have fun, *bachchaas*,' he said. 'Make sure all of you have your phones on you, please. Don't wander away like you always do… Oh, and don't be *toooo* naughty!' he ended with a wink.

'Thanks, Happy Uncle,' said Ansh, taking the basket from him with an excited smile. He did love this food, especially when compared to his mom's. Suddenly, he felt something slithering wetly down his arm towards the basket. 'Eek!' he screeched, his heart thumping loudly. But it was only the elephant who had come up behind him.

A grey trunk sniffed hungrily before tossing a fresh bread roll into its mouth.

'Knock it off, Elfu!' exclaimed Rohan. He looked apologetically at Ansh. 'Erm, Elfu loves human food. One of his many eccentricities. But he's harmless, really.' He gave a stern look to Elfu, who turned his head defiantly.

Ansh glowered at the animal, muttering 'pesky elephant' under his breath.

• • • • • • • • • • • • •

The party of five set off towards the back of the resort. They passed a large kitchen garden with neat square patches that showed off spinach and herbs, creepers of *lauki* and fat red tomatoes. They walked through an enormous fruit orchard with trees laden with mangoes, papayas, *chikus*, guavas and bananas, until they finally reached a fence with a rickety wooden gate.

Elfu had to squeeze through the gate before they could set off into the dark green forest beyond. They crossed trees and shrubs as they trudged along the faint path that had worn away. As they reached a canopy of tall bamboo, Rohan asked curiously, 'Hey, where are we going anyway?'

Ansh smiled mysteriously. 'You'll see. You like water, don't you?'

Just as he said that, Rohan heard it. It sounded like it was raining heavily. As he turned the corner, he realized they had come upon a small clearing. He gazed upon a large pool of greenish water, about the size of an Olympic swimming pool. On the left, a small waterfall emptied into it from about twenty feet above. On the other side, large round rocks kept most of the water in the basin, though some of it escaped and flowed out as a narrow, boulder-strewn creek. The pool was surrounded by lush tropical greenery, giving it the feel of a rainforest. The entire scene looked made-up, like a landscape painting from an artist's imagination.

Rohan grinned from ear to ear. 'This is amazing, guys! Just like at home in Kerala!'

Meanwhile, Noor had whipped off her dress and jumped into the pool with a loud whoop.

Zoya followed her a little more sedately, telling Rohan, 'Don't worry, it's quite safe. It's not very deep as the waterfall is fed mostly by rainfall. As there are no currents, and we're all strong swimmers, the parental units don't mind…too much, that is.'

Ansh muttered as he gingerly sidled in, 'Why is this pool always so muddy? I'll have to shower again when we get back.'

'There goes the Big City Boy again,' mocked Noor.

Thrilled to bits at seeing so much water, Elfu pushed past Ansh and waded happily into the pool.

'Oi! If you come in, all the water will go out,' exclaimed Ansh, looking annoyed.

Elfu ignored him. In the flash of an eye, the elephant forcefully sprayed a trunkful of water at Ansh, who sank down right into the pool!

• • • • • • • • • • • • •

3

'Aargh!' spluttered Ansh, struggling to rise as water streamed down his face while the others splashed around in hysterical laughter. Soon, there was a rollicking water fight between the children and the elephant.

After a while, Zoya said, 'I'm hungry. Let's see if Elfu has left anything for us!'

The children sneaked out, leaving Elfu playing blissfully under the waterfall. They laid a plastic sheet on the rocks near the pool and opened the picnic basket.

'Goanese *poi* bread! Yum! Banana chips, fish cutlets – don't worry, Ansh, there is vegetarian *methyeche pole* – methi dosa – for you. Oh, wow! There's bebinca too!' Zoya said the last name with a sigh of rapture. She just adored this very Goan dessert – a seven-layered pudding made with coconut milk, eggs, butter and jaggery.

As they were tucking in happily, Elfu suddenly realized he was missing out on the action and waded over. Rohan looked amused as the elephant turned his beseeching eyes on the other children by turns. They were no match for his pleading expression, and Noor was the first to crack and offer him some *poi*.

'Drama king,' muttered Rohan affectionately.

Ansh brought out his mum's creation and offered it hopefully to Elfu. *This annoying animal will be worth something if he eats the monstrosities that mum dishes up regularly*, he thought. Ansh felt too guilty to throw away food and invariably had to stuff it down himself. Stupid conscience!

Elfu looked at the crumbly, dry, dull-looking cake made of crushed chickpeas, flaxseed and oats for a moment, before turning his head away disdainfully and extending his trunk towards Zoya and Noor. *Oh well*, thought Ansh mournfully, *I tried*.

As the kids lay back on the picnic sheet, replete and relaxed, Ansh took out his phone and started sketching the scene on a drawing app. After a bit, he hollered, 'Who's up for some cricket? Rohan?' turning his head to the older boy, hopefully.

'Nah, I'm more into hiking and rock climbing…but you know who *has* learnt to hold a bat?' He signalled towards Elfu, who was grazing lazily off the trees.

'What?' exclaimed Ansh incredulously, looking at the elephant with new, though reluctant, respect.

'Well, he's hardly Tendulkar or Kohli, but he sometimes connects if you throw the ball slowly enough,' said Rohan.

'This we have to see!' exclaimed Noor and jumped up.

Soon Elfu's trunk was wrapped awkwardly around a bat, and everyone was taking turns throwing the ball to him. After missing the first few times, Elfu connected with the ball so hard that it went flying over Zoya's head and disappeared into the bushes at the side of the waterfall.

Ansh looked on in despair and wailed, 'N-o-o-o! No, no, no, no! Ma is going to kill me! This is the fifth ball

I've lost this month. She threatened that there would be no more cricket balls in my future, ever, if I lost this one.'

Noor rolled her eyes, saying, 'Chill, we'll find it,' and bounded off. As the others followed her, she called back, 'I see it... Hang on.'

As they caught up with Noor, they saw the ball half-hidden on a slight slope, behind some brambles. All of them exchanged looks.

Ansh looked at Zoya and said, 'You go.'

Zoya retorted, 'No, you go.'

Rohan stood up taller and was about to offer to get the ball back when Noor rushed past him, saying, 'Oi, I'll go, what's there to be scared of?' She stepped down and suddenly slithered out of view.

The others rushed to peer over and saw her standing a few feet below. She had, somehow, slipped through the dense bushes and was now sitting on a narrow stone path that led to a dark opening in the rock face. 'Guys! Come down here...' she said. 'I think it's a hidden cave! Be careful. It's slippery! Let Elfu come first.'

She stood to the side as Rohan tried to egg Elfu on, who longingly turned his head back towards the waterfall. Finally, after many 'Good boys', 'Brave boys' and 'You can do its', Elfu accepted that he was not about to gain his freedom anytime soon and lumbered down ungraciously, trampling the bushes and clearing the path ahead for the others.

Soon, they were at the mouth of a damp, dark cave, looking nervously at each other. Rohan moved to the front of the group and said, 'Let me go first. I've done some spelunking in Meghalaya with Dad. We won't go in more than a hundred feet... We will need proper equipment beyond that.'

'Splzzaa...what?' asked Ansh.

Zoya asked in a vaguely puzzled tone, 'Oh, you don't know about it? It's really interesting. It's when you go exploring deep inside caves. It can be quite dangerous, actually.' She smiled at Rohan for confirmation.

'Okayyyyy, Professor Zo, thanks for the daily lesson,' chimed in Ansh and Noor together, smiling cheekily at her. She rolled her eyes and smiled back at them.

Rohan switched on his phone torch and entered the cave cautiously. Elfu held on to his shirt with his trunk and followed him hesitantly, barely squeezing through, while the others trailed behind them. To their relief, the cave immediately opened into a sizeable room-like structure before narrowing into a passageway at the back. Though faint greenish light was filtering into the cave through the waterfall, the children had their phone torches on, and four beams of light began to dance around the cave.

They walked on for a few moments when Rohan shouted, 'Look! Over here...drawings on the walls! Insane! Somebody must have lived here once.'

The others rushed over and started peering at the paintings. Their eyes goggled at what they saw. There were herds of bison and deer running, with hunters pursuing them. There was even a rhinoceros.

Zoya exclaimed loudly, 'O.M.G! I think I'm going to faint! These might be prehistoric! Last year, I wrote a report on the Bhimbetka cave paintings for a project. These look like those.'

Noor called out from the back. 'Look! There's a drawing of an elephant with a star mark on its forehead... just like Elfu!'

Everyone gathered around Noor, with Elfu following close behind. His grip on Rohan's shirt was as firm as ever.

'Shhh,' said Rohan, stroking his trunk comfortingly. 'Don't worry, Elfu Master. There's nothing to be scared of.'

Four lights trained on a crude line drawing of an elephant whose only distinguishing feature was a five-pointed star on its forehead. A group of people was shown bowing before it.

Elfu looked at it wonderingly. Letting go of Rohan's arm, he lifted his trunk and sniffed the elephant in the picture. As his trunk touched the star on its forehead, there was a spark and hiss. The lights on all the phones went out.

• • • • • • • • • • • • •

'Hello! What's happening?' yelped Ansh at the sudden darkness in the cave.

Just as suddenly as they had switched off, all four phones lit up again with an eerie blue light.

An electronic voice boomed haltingly, 'App. Downloading. Now.' Concentric circles appeared on the screens, indicating the percentage downloaded.

The children stood still. They involuntarily clutched each other's hands fiercely. Elfu's trunk snaked around Rohan's waist, seeking comfort. As the download finished, an icon of an elephant head with a five-pointed star appeared on each phone.

The voice boomed again, 'Download. Completed. Press. Anywhere. To. Start.'

Just as Zoya said, 'Wait. Everyone, let's discuss this first – ', Noor pressed the icon on her phone firmly.

'No!' screeched Rohan and Zoya while Ansh stood frozen in horror. But it was too late.

There was a buzzing sound that steadily increased in volume. The wind picked up speed, and it seemed like a strobe light was flashing in the cave. Suddenly, everything began to spin. The children felt weightless as though they were hurtling down a high roller-coaster.

'Hold on, everyone!' screamed Ansh, extending his hands to try and grab whoever he could.

Then, everything went silent.

• • • • • • • • • • • • •

4

The children slowly opened their eyes.

Ansh said faintly, 'It's light now.' As they looked around, they realized they were no longer inside the dark cave. In fact, they were someplace they had never been before – a vast, muddy open field next to a wide, flowing river. The stench was indescribable. As they looked around in shock, they saw crowds and crowds of men everywhere.

Rohan exclaimed, 'Look! They are all dressed up for a play.' He pointed to the many men lying on the ground, groaning theatrically with fake blood smeared across their faces and bodies. Others seemed to be playing dead.

Zoya said, 'Hey, look up ahead. Those guys are in skirts! They kind of look like ancient Romans, but…' She pointed a little distance away to where two groups of men stood before a small stage to which finishing touches were being put hastily.

The first group was wearing skirts with boots, some sort of stiff leather shirts and helmets. They were holding the longest spears Zoya had ever seen – almost twenty feet in length, nearly four times her height!

The other group looked sad and frightened, yet as though they were trying to keep their chins up. They were Indians wearing tightly wound knee-length dhotis, cotton tunics with leather straps criss-crossing their chests, leather belts around their waists and strange-looking turbans with large knots that rested just above their foreheads. Their shields, spears, swords, bows and arrows were stacked up in a big pile close by.

Eknoor whispered, 'This is surreal! Are we on a movie set?'

A short man in a military-skirt costume strode onto the stage. He started speaking loudly. The language sounded alien to the children, but they realized they could understand it, although it felt like it was coming from a distance.

Then, suddenly, Ansh let out a screech. 'Guys! Look at yourselves! Our clothes have changed!' Everyone looked down and noted incredulously that they too were dressed like the Indian group, in dhotis and tunics, with leather straps across their chests.

Rohan felt something tight around his head. He put his hand up to check and was shocked to find a little-too-snug turban. Looking down he saw they all had strappy sandals on their feet and small cloth pouches hanging off their sides.

Zoya drifted into a trance. She scrabbled through her pouch and sighed with relief as she pulled out her phone from it. 'Thank heavens,' she muttered.

'Oh…there's no signal!' she said next, followed by, 'Uff, thank God I persuaded Ammi to subscribe to the Children's History app for offline access.' She started typing furiously. Finally, she turned around to look at the others. Taking a deep breath, she held up the phone to them. 'Guys. I don't

know how to say this, but…err…I mean…I think we are…'
She looked like she was going to have a fit.

'What is it, Zoya?' asked Rohan kindly. 'You can tell us.'

'I think we are actually in the past…and that is Alexander the Great in front of us!' The words rushed out all jumbled – Zoya couldn't believe how absurd she sounded.

'What rubbish!' burst out Ansh. 'How can we be…' he caught sight of Zoya's phone. He saw a painting labelled *'Artist's interpretation of Indian King Porus and Alexander the Great meeting after the Battle of Hydaspes in 326 BCE'.*

He looked down at his dhoti and sandals, then looked up at the stage. The others also looked down at themselves, and then up at the stage. Horrified looks began to dawn on their faces. It was all too clear – they WERE stuck in the past. These people weren't actors. They were wounded soldiers. That was real blood, and the dead soldiers were… actually dead! Those were not fake horses and elephants lying on the ground.

Zoya started whispering furiously. 'Okay, so what I remember is that Alexander the Great wanted to conquer the world. He began from the small Greek kingdom of Macedonia and annihilated the Persian Empire in something like ten years. Here we are at the Battle… of… Hy-dasssspes? Oh, wait… It's the Jhelum river!'

Rohan said with a frown, 'But the Jhelum is in Pakistan.'

Noor had started to recover her spirit. 'Wait, what? Are we in Pakistan right now? Insane!'

Zoya broke in, 'Well, it won't become Pakistan for another 2,000 years, so calm yourself!'

Suddenly there was some activity up front. The wounded King Porus was led onto the stage. He was a giant of a man – Rohan reckoned at least six feet nine inches, with an arrow sticking out of his arm! Elfu looked at his scrawny trunk and then at Porus's massive arm enviously. Alexander, who was five feet nothing, looked like a dwarf in front of Porus, barely reaching his chest.

Alexander cleared his throat and said, 'Well, O Porus? What is to be done with you? You have been a worthy opponent. How should we treat you, I wonder?'

An Indian man standing next to Alexander translated

his speech so that Porus would understand. Though it felt like the voices they heard were passing through water before reaching their ears, the children could understand this language as well.

Ansh whispered, 'Hey, this sounds a lot like the chanting my mum does every morning.'

'You're right,' said Zoya with a thoughtful look. 'They might be speaking in Sanskrit.'

Just as Porus began to reply, the kids chanted in unison along with him, 'Then treat me like a king, O Alexander!' To their surprise, they had spoken in the same Indian language as Porus!

'Wait! How did you know what he was going to say?'

The group turned around to see a handsome youth of about sixteen. He was lean and tall with piercingly intelligent eyes. A long, curly black mane fell below his shoulders. Rohan looked enviously at the boy's muscled physique, which had clearly been honed by a lot of working out.

The youth gazed at them curiously as he asked, 'You don't look like you're from around here. Who are you, and where are you from?'

'Err...' mumbled Zoya.

They were caught!

• • • • • • • • • • • • • •

5

They could hardly tell this unknown boy that they were from the future! They themselves were finding it hard to believe.

Noor had a flash of inspiration. 'We are from a land far, far…extremely far away…from the south, you know.'

Thankfully for them, Alexander started speaking again, and they all turned to look at the stage.

Alexander was looking at Porus with admiration.

'What spirit! Even injured and at a disadvantage like this, you demand honour!' He held out his arms and said, 'O King, come, let us be partners. We will conquer the world together.' As they hugged, the short-statured Alexander's face was squashed into Porus's chest. It was a ludicrous sight.

The unknown youth looked at the four children and said, 'Ahh…Dakshin Bharat. I have heard so many tales of that place. I would love to visit one day…if my teacher ever gives me leave.' He sighed. 'I am Chandragupta, Chandragupta Maurya,' he said with a smile. 'And what are you all doing so far away from home?'

Zoya's eyes started bulging in amazement when she heard the name while Rohan stammered, 'Well…

actually...' He was desperately trying to think up a reason when there was a commotion up ahead.

By now, Porus had been escorted off the stage. Alexander was sitting next to a pure black horse lying lifeless on the ground. Weirdly enough, the horse's head looked like a cow's, and there was a white star mark on its forehead. Tears were streaming from Alexander's eyes.

'What is happening?' whispered Noor. 'Why is he crying? I'm so confused...'

Chandragupta turned to her with an exasperated tut. 'His horse died,' he said. 'This Yavana twerp is the oversentimental sort. A bit too in touch with his emotions if you know what I mean. Looking at how he cries over every little thing, you'd never imagine his absolute ferociousness on the battleground. I've heard he's never lost a battle in his life...' He sounded glum.

Meanwhile, Alexander was moaning, 'O Bucephalus! My old friend, you've been by my side since I was thirteen... What will I do without you? How can I bear to ride another steed?' He began weeping in earnest, laying his head on the dead horse's neck as his generals went and stood protectively behind him.

When Alexander finally stood up, eyes red, back straight, and still hiccupping sporadically, he proclaimed, 'I declare that a new city shall be raised near here. It will be named after my beloved horse – Alexandria Bucephala. And so my loyal four-legged friend will be remembered eternally.'

A Greek soldier standing close to the children sniggered to his neighbour, 'Another one? Don't we have enough Alexandrias already?'

'Twenty in the last eight years,' retorted his friend with a short laugh. 'Perhaps our Great Leader could name a few cities after his loyal soldiers once in a while.'

Rohan, though, was touched by Alexander's devotion. He turned to Elfu and told him misty-eyed, 'I love you, Elfu-pelfu. When you're gone, I'll definitely name a place after you, even if it's just a small neighbourhood park. After all, we can't all be world conquerors.'

Elfu let out a scandalized harrumph and stepped back hastily. Death? Why was Rohan talking about killing him? He was still a kid! He had places to go and treats to eat.

Uneasy, Elfu wandered off on his own. Up ahead, he saw a herd of the world's largest elephants. Ooh! Other Elfus to play with, he thought excitedly. But when he went up to them, he realized they were massive brutes – almost twice his size – and not particularly friendly. Their tusks were nearly as long as Elfu was tall, and they were covered in nasty-looking metal spikes. They had metal armour around their battle-scarred legs and very uncomfortable-looking structures on their backs. These even had people sitting in them. Just looking at them made Elfu's back scratch and ache.

Then he saw a gigantic elephant covered in sparkly metal and jewels glaring at him; five or six big arrows were sticking out of him at various places. Oh, it also had a star mark on its forehead! Excited at this discovery, Elfu approached him.

It harrumphed to him, 'Pesky little calf! What are you doing here among your elders and betters? Go back to your mother!'

Elfu sidled back up to Rohan, trying to ineffectually hide behind him. 'I'm fine here. I don't really need anyone else to play with,' he squeaked to himself.

When the kids turned around, they saw that Chandragupta was patting Elfu's trunk. The elephant was bowing his head lower and lower. His eyes were shut, and he looked like he would topple over in relaxed bliss. If there was an elephant heaven, Elfu was in it at that moment.

Chandragupta said affectionately, 'I love animals. And they seem to love me back. Somehow, they always listen to me.'

The children were so engrossed in their conversation, they had lost track of their surroundings. Suddenly, Ansh started to surreptitiously kick Noor. As she turned her head to snap at him, her eyes widened. The group heard a loud voice exclaiming in Greek, 'Over here!'

The children were surrounded by Greek soldiers, whose long spears were pointing dangerously at them. They were looking at Elfu suspiciously. 'Whose elephant is this?' they demanded to know. 'Don't you know that all war elephants belong to our commander, the mighty Alexander?'

The children gulped. They were in for it now, especially poor Elfu!

• • • • • • • • • • • • •

6

After a few panic-stricken moments, Chandragupta came to the front and replied in broken Greek, 'No! You make big mistake. This…is… dwarf elephant. Cursed. See this? Mark on forehead very unlucky. You don't want. We take him…sacrifice…to Takshashila.'

At this, the Greek soldiers backed away quickly, making signs to ward off evil.

Chandragupta wiped his brow in relief. He turned to the others and said in Sanskrit, 'Well! It's good that they believed me, or else it would have been the end of your elephant. They are in great demand nowadays with the wars going on.' He noticed Elfu glaring at him. He went up to him and whispered, 'No, my *gaja*, I didn't mean to call you a cursed one. It was just to get those wicked men away from you.' Elfu quickly relented, nudging him with his trunk for more cuddles.

Stroking Elfu's trunk, Chandragupta said, 'Okay, we all need to leave the battlefield…NOW! It's not safe here. I must head back to Takshashila. My guru will be waiting for a full report of the battle – he sent me here to observe the Yavana battle strategies. Where are you headed?'

Rohan had thought up the perfect cover story.

'Well, as you know, we are from the far south,' he said. 'We are four brothers who have been orphaned recently.' He glared warningly at Noor as she opened her mouth to shout at him for making her a boy. 'Our father was a scholar who always said that Takshashila was the best place in the world for education. So, that's where we are going.'

Chandragupta exclaimed, 'Great! Why don't you come with me? It's about a day's walk from here on foot, though I rode. My horse is tethered in those trees over there. Oh, and we will have to spend the night in the forest on the way.'

Ansh whispered anxiously to Noor, 'We need to get back to our own time!'

Zoya looked perturbed yet thoughtful.

Rohan saw their faces and turned to Chandragupta. 'If you don't mind, I need a few moments with my brothers in private.' He led his friends away from Chandragupta.

'Rohan, what are you doing?' Noor's whisper sounded like a snake's hiss. 'We need to get back. Not get into more complications!'

'We need to go back home, now!' Ansh added in an almost-wail.

Rohan whispered hurriedly, 'I thought it would be safer for us to go into a town and figure out our next steps. This battlefield is no place for us. It will get dark soon, and we have no skills to survive. There are dangerous, armed soldiers everywhere. I didn't mean...'

Zoya interrupted, 'Rohan is right, guys. We do need to get home, but staying here in the middle of nowhere, with all these dead people around us, isn't going to help.' A part of her was quite curious to see Takshashila, but she would never admit that out loud.

Noor paused. Looking around at all the death and destruction, she gave a slight nod and said, 'Okay.'

Though Ansh looked mutinous, he nodded silently.

As the children turned to return to the youth, they were stopped by Zoya. She whispered rapidly, 'Wait! Do you guys realize who that is? It's Chandragupta Maurya, the first emperor in history to unite India! Emperor Ashoka's grandfather! I think I'm going to faint.'

The other children gazed at the youth's pleasant expression.

'Doesn't seem like the face of a soon-to-be ferocious conqueror to me,' Noor muttered wonderingly.

• • • • • • • • • • • • •

Soon, the party began its journey. Chandragupta was leading the horse by its reins, walking alongside the children. They were going along the riverbank when the youth turned to Zoya, who was next to him, and said, 'Actually, there is a straightforward road to Takshashila – the ancient Uttarapath – normally, I would take that. I am sure you've heard of it.'

When he saw her nod, he continued, 'Well, I think we should avoid it at all costs right now – the Greeks are still on a rampage, and if they see the horse and the elephant, they will commandeer them for sure.'

Rohan piped up from behind. 'Yes, yes. In that case, we should definitely take another route... So, which one?'

Pointing at a narrow point in the river, Chandragupta said, 'Well, we will have to cross the river and take the little-used forest path, but you'll be quite safe with me.'

The children could see some people at the riverbank up ahead. A couple of boatmen were lazing in their moored boats and chatting. Chandragupta ignored them and kept walking rapidly ahead before coming to a stop. As the children caught up, they saw the strangest sight. There was a dead buffalo floating upside-down in the river...and it seemed to be inflated! A rope was tied to one of its blown-up legs, and a man squatting on the riverbank held the rope's free end.

Noor screeched, 'What is that? A *bhainsa* balloon? Look at what that other guy is doing!'

The man's companion was squatting next to him, blowing air with his mouth into another buffalo skin through a hole in one of its hooves!

All the children thought this was disgusting, especially Ansh, who started turning a little green in the face.

Meanwhile, Chandragupta had walked up to the first man and asked, 'We need to cross... How much?'

The man looked from Chandragupta to the children, then at the animals.

''Xtra for th' horse and ellie,' he said lazily.

Meanwhile, the children's faces looked more and more horrified by the minute. Surely, Chandragupta could not be thinking of...

Chandragupta had finished his amiable negotiation and turned to the children. 'Let's go!' he yelled.

They looked at him with thunderstruck expressions.

'How?' exclaimed Noor. 'On the *bhainsa* balloon?'

He replied with a small chuckle, 'Well, yes. That's all we can afford. Acharya doesn't give me a large allowance.'

He removed the pouch hanging from his waist and tied it securely to his turban before wading into the river. He tied the horse's lead to a foreleg of one of the buffalo-floats and firmly grasped another leg with one hand.

Mimicking him, the children also tied their pouches around their turbans hesitantly. Zoya whispered worriedly, 'My phone better not get ruined.'

They kept looking at Chandragupta reluctantly until, filled with trepidation, Noor followed him into the river and held another one of the buffalo skin's inflated legs. Zoya went in next and grasped the third leg. Rohan approached the second buffalo-float, urging Elfu along into the water. This wasn't hard, as Elfu loved swimming. Ansh was the last and most reluctant one to join.

Two men came and started leading the buffalo-floats briskly into the swollen waters of the Jhelum.

The children held on as they waded and stumbled over rough stones, and the current tried to carry them downstream. The other side seemed awfully far away. The river deepened suddenly, and everyone was forced to start swimming awkwardly with one hand, clutching on to their float for dear life with the other.

Elfu was swimming by himself, but gently held a foreleg of the dead buffalo in his trunk out of solidarity. On the whole, the group was quite relieved when they staggered onto the riverbank on the far side.

Chandragupta turned and laughed when he saw the wet and bedraggled children. He said kindly, 'Don't worry, you'll dry off soon.' He started walking towards the trees, leading his horse by its reins. Elfu stayed as close to him as possible, and the children walked a little behind. A little peeved at Elfu's desertion, Rohan caught up with the other lad. They soon entered a dark, heavily wooded area with massive trees all around.

Leading the way onto a narrow dirt path worn away due to use, Chandragupta said, 'We have a couple more hours to go before darkness falls, and then we stop for the night. We should reach Takshashila by tomorrow evening.'

Following them at a slower place, Ansh, Zoya and Noor were lost in thought, taking in the surroundings.

Ansh said nervously, 'Um, how are we going to get home? I knew that pesky elephant would do us no good!'

'Stop blaming poor Elfu for everything,' Noor retorted. 'Isn't this a part of the Punjab?' she asked, looking around wonderingly.

'Yep,' answered Zoya absently, busy doing something on her phone.

'My ancestral place!' Noor squealed excitedly. 'But aren't there too many trees here? Where are the unending mustard fields? The *makki* ki roti? Yum! I'm hungry.'

Zoya looked up. '*Makki* is corn, which came from the Americas,' she said. 'It won't reach India for another 1,800 years, until the Portuguese arrive.' She continued to absent-mindedly browse the Children's History app as she walked.

Chandragupta caught a glimpse of her phone and exclaimed, 'Oh! What is that? I've never seen anything like this before.'

Zoya thought fast and replied, 'Erm, this is a speciality of…south India, you know. It helps us calculate sums and remember things.'

Chandragupta saw the letters of the English alphabet scattered across the screen and said curiously, 'And this script? I've never seen a *lipi* like this before.'

'Oh, that's from our particular village that has its own script.' Zoya hastily thrust the phone back in her pouch. *Out of sight, out of mind*, she thought hopefully. 'Anyway, tell us about yourself – have you grown up around here?' she asked Chandragupta. She already knew he was from Bihar, though…a long, long way from there.

Chandragupta said, 'I come from the mighty *mahajanapada* of Magadha – far to the east…where the cruel Dhanananda rules. He is the most powerful king that ever was.'

No…that's going to be you, thought Zoya with a mental chuckle.

Chandragupta continued, 'I was brought to Takshashila by my guru to study to become a king.'

I bet, Zoya sniggered to herself.

'And how long have you been with Acharya Chanakya…?' As the words slipped out, Zoya's cheeks grew bright red. The cat was out of the bag.

Chandragupta stared at her with an arrested expression. 'How do you know my guru's name?'

'Well...his fame has spread even to the south...' she replied weakly, trying to sound convincing. 'So, I assumed you must be learning from him as he is said to be the best in Takshashila.'

Noor gave her a dirty look and jumped in. 'So, tell me, Chandu, how come there are so many trees and forests here? I thought there would be many more fields for farming?'

'*Chandu*? Really?' he asked, raising his eyebrows incredulously. 'Well, this area is known for its dense forests. You will see tree trunks so wide that even four men can't encircle them with joined hands!'

Noor thought of all the Hindi movies showing the flat, treeless plains of Punjab and rolled her eyes in amazement.

As the children walked along, chatting away, the hot and humid monsoon weather started catching up with them. Sweat began to run down from their brows. Ansh was the first to wilt. He started to walk slower and slower, until Noor turned back and said, 'Well, a snail is going to overtake you soon.'

'It's hot! And I'm tired! And I want water!' he cried.

'Just a little further,' said Zoya encouragingly.

'I. Want. To. Go. Home. On a plane. Now!' screamed Ansh, reaching the very end of his tether. 'I want my car and my air conditioner and my own bed. I want my mamma!'

The others looked on, hearts pounding, as Chandragupta started frowning heavily at these unfamiliar words.

Rohan, Zoya and Noor turned horrified faces towards Ansh. This time, the game was well and truly up.

• • • • • • • • • • • •

7

Chandragupta stared into Ansh's face and turned to Rohan. In a worried tone, he asked, 'Playn? Arkondishner? Kaar? What are these things that he wants?'

Rohan was at a total loss for words. As he was figuring out how to reply, his eyes fell on Elfu, lazily chomping on some leaves. He replied quickly, 'Oh, those are our pets at home! My brother is very attached to them, you know. He misses them terribly...'

Chandragupta could relate to this. 'Yes, I too love animals. What kind of pets are these?'

Seeing Rohan struggle to answer, Noor replied, 'Oh! These are very special pets. Very special, indeed.'

'Car is very fast!' said Noor, making a zooming gesture with her hand. 'It overtakes everyone, left and right. Plane is a large flying bird... My brother here keeps wanting to take it for a ride!' She slapped Ansh on the back playfully.

When she saw Zoya trying to suppress a snigger, she hammed it up even more.

'And air conditioner...where do I begin about that one? I would love to have it here right now! Sometimes, we all just stand and wait for it to breathe on us...' she sighed, thinking wistfully of her aircon at home.

Chandragupta was looking very perplexed. *Large birds that can give people rides? And I love animals, but I have never, ever wanted any of them to breathe on me. Curiouser and curiouser,* he thought. Shaking his head in disbelief, he took a deep breath and said soothingly to Ansh, 'Come, let's find you some water. You'll feel better.'

Chandragupta cocked his ear first in one direction and then another. Then, he led them to a clear stream. He took out a thin cloth from his pouch and dipped it, straining the water through it into a small leather flask. Meanwhile, his horse began lapping thirstily at the water.

'Here, have some,' he offered Ansh. The boy looked at the pouch as if it were the devil.

'That! You want me to drink that…stream…' words failed Ansh. He burst out, 'Can we get Bisleri from somewhere?'

Zoya gave Ansh an awful glare as Chandragupta looked puzzled. 'Bish-leri? What is that?' he asked.

'Oh, we have a special stream called Bisleri in our village – everyone gets their drinking water from there. We're not in the south anymore, brother. Drink this quietly…' Zoya said, giving Ansh another meaningful look.

Ansh quietened down and sipped the water sulkily. *Hey, this is refreshing,* he thought. *Tastes just like the posh water bottled from mountain streams for the resort guests! And I'm getting it for free!*

• • • • • • • • • • • •

The journey seemed to take ages. Dense shrubs made the going hard, and only faint, speckled sunlight filtered through the tall trees. A mulchy, musty smell permeated the air. There was constant movement around them as rabbits, porcupines and other small animals scurried around in the undergrowth.

'Ah!' shrieked Zoya, 'I think I just squashed something!'

They all stopped briefly to look at the remains of a large, juicy insect that had had an unfortunate encounter with Zoya's sandal.

'Don't look down, just keep walking,' advised Rohan.

'Ugh,' said Zoya in agreement, and looked straight ahead with determination and continued on.

As the sun started its rapid descent, birds began cheeping louder and louder, until the noise was deafening.

Chandragupta soon said, 'Normally, I would have ridden straight through, but let's stop here for the night.' He pointed to a little grove of trees. He had been collecting twigs as he walked. Soon, he had a merry little fire going. 'There! That should keep the creepy-crawlies away,' he said with satisfaction.

'Creepy-crawlies?' repeated Ansh nervously. 'What kind and just how many are we talking about?'

Chandragupta's laughter echoed through the forest.

'Don't worry, my young friend. Just make yourself comfortable. I'll take the first watch to make sure you come to no harm...from robbers and tigers and things that crawl!'

'What are we going to eat?' Zoya wondered aloud.

'Well, I have some roasted chana that we can share,' he replied. 'Typical travel food. And there's mangoes,' he added, pointing to the trees around them.

'What? There are mangoes here?' shouted Rohan happily.

Chandragupta replied 'Look around you. It's summer. There are mangoes everywhere!'

Sure enough, as they peered up in the gloomy twilight, they realized that they were in fact standing right in the middle of a mango grove! Endless trees bowing low with the weight of heavy mangoes as far as the eye could see. Suddenly, they noticed that Elfu was already delightedly plucking and flinging whole mangoes into his mouth.

With a whoop of delight, they started grabbing mangoes, biting off the tips and squeezing the pulp and juice into their mouths. They thoroughly enjoyed their messy feast. Soon, everyone, including Elfu, was in a mango-binge-induced coma.

Chandragupta squatted down in front of the fire with his sword resting between his legs.

Noor volunteered, 'I can take the next watch, Chandu. I'm not scared.'

Chandragupta smiled and said 'Okay, I will wake you up after one *prahar*.'

Zoya whispered to the others, 'That means three hours.'

Noor smiled back, lay down on the bare ground close to Chandragupta and was soon out like a light.

The others were slow to follow, looking at the hard forest ground reluctantly for a few moments before lying down. Rohan gazed up, observing the twinkling of the fireflies drowsily. His eyes drifted shut as he listened to the sounds of the jungle with contentment – the rustling noises of small animals as they moved through the grass, the desultory cheeping of birds as they settled in for the night.

Zoya lay back and thought longingly of her dinner. Mangoes were all very well, but Ammi was planning to make biryani today, and she adored biryani. Sleepily, she reflected on the past few hours. *I can't believe what is happening...is this a dream?* With these thoughts, she surrendered to sleep.

Ansh had the hardest time nodding off. The ground was hard and scratchy. He was sure he could see a thousand bright eyes peering at him from all sides. He missed his bed in his room where there were no insects or animals lurking around. *I need to get back to Ma*, he thought. *She must be panicking by now. How will we ever get back?* Despite his worries, his eyes finally closed.

• • • • • • • • • • • • •

Noor woke up with a start when there was a light tap on her shoulder. She sat up sleepily, as Chandragupta whispered, 'I've added some wood to the fire – wake me if there's any problem.'

'Don't worry, Chandu, I've got this,' she whispered back confidently. *I do love adventures*, she thought as she poked a stick into the fire and stared at the hypnotic dancing flames. *This is such fu...*'

Noor awoke with a start when she heard a hiss. Pale streaks of light were lighting the sky. The fire was out, and only smouldering embers remained. There was an enormous cobra sitting up in front of her, its hood fanned out in a terrifying threat!

• • • • • • • • • • • • •

8

'Err, Chandu…' Noor whispered desperately, trying to reach behind with her arm while not moving. Her heart started pounding heavily.

'Chandu, wake up!' Noor spoke louder this time.

Meanwhile, the snake had started swaying from side to side. It was not a comforting sight.

Chandragupta awoke and took the scene in. He said in a low voice from behind Noor, 'Calm down, and whatever you do, don't move.' Then, he crept away and appeared behind the snake. He started making some gentle tapping noises with his feet. *Rat-a-tat-a tat-a-tat.* The snake slowly turned away from Noor and faced Chandragupta. The youth changed the rhythm of the tapping as he backed away slowly. Suddenly, the snake lay flat on the ground, and after looking at him with its beady eyes for a few moments, slithered away quietly.

Small snores were still emanating from the group.

'Phew!' said Noor weakly. 'You saved our hides…again!'

'It's nothing,' replied Chandragupta. 'Our village has a lot of snakes. I picked up this trick from the snake charmer. I'm glad it worked because I didn't have any others up my sleeve...'

• • • • • • • • • • • • •

As soon as everyone was up, Noor excitedly described the incident with the snake. Once they had washed up in the nearby stream, the group resumed their journey.

The four friends learnt about Chandragupta's life – how he never knew his father, how he'd been raised by a cowherd to protect him from his family's enemies and how he used to work for a hunter.

'Acharya reckons I'll be ready soon,' Chandragupta said confidently. 'We'll smash that Nanda rascal, and I can restore my family honour.' Then he pointed into the distance in front of them. 'Ah, look!' he exclaimed. 'We are near the outskirts. Not far now.'

They saw the dense forest ending up ahead with open spaces beyond. Soon, they joined a broad, mud-beaten road and started walking along it, passing lush green fields of newly sown rice on either side.

Thank heavens, thought Zoya. She wouldn't admit it, especially to Ansh, but she was also nearing the end of her tether. She hadn't exercised as much the whole of the last year as she had in these last twenty-four hours!

'Tell us more about your guru,' urged Zoya, trying to get her mind off her leaden feet and aching body.

'As you may know, he goes by many names,' Chandragupta said. 'His birth name is Vishnugupta, but I call him Acharya Chanakya. He is a renowned Brahmin professor of political science. A few years ago, he went to the court of the Nanda king and was insulted horribly. The king didn't even rise to receive him, much less invite him in and wash his feet. In fact, that crass man laughed at the Acharya's looks!' Chandragupta trembled with outrage.

'Acharya is not...well...the calmest of people, and he took a deadly vow there and then that he would not rest until he had brought down the whole dynasty. Dhanananda was furious, but even he was too scared to commit the sin of murdering a Brahmin.'

As the others looked puzzled, Zoya gave them a warning look and said, 'Of course, of course. That would be unthinkable.'

She whispered to the others in English, 'In ancient India, people believed that if you killed a Brahmin, you would be cursed forever.'

Chandragupta continued, 'Acharya wandered the land looking for someone to be his champion but couldn't find anyone for the longest time. Then one day, as he was passing my village, he saw me play-acting with my mates. I was pretending to be king – holding court, and deciding who was right and who was wrong. That was when I was working for the hunter. Acharya asked me a few questions and then, before I knew it, he was asking my master's permission to take me with him and make me a warrior. Imagine! Me! We are just poor folk. So, here I am.'

'Do you live with him all the time?' asked Noor curiously.

'Yes, I've been living with him in Takshashila these last few years,' Chandragupta replied with a quizzical expression.

After a moment's pause, he said, 'Is it different in the south? In Takshashila, all students live with their teachers like a family until they are deemed ready to go out into the world.'

None of them had an answer for his question.

'How is it? Living with the Acharya?' asked Noor abruptly, trying to change the topic.

'Acharya Chanakya can be scary and quite hard to say no to. And does he work me hard...there is no rest!' said Chandragupta, but his voice was laced with admiration. 'But he is the best teacher ever!'

'Hmm,' said Ansh dubiously, thinking of all his scary teachers at school. He was glad he got to go home to his mum every day.

It was late afternoon when they reached the outskirts of a town. The road had gotten quite busy. There were dozens of pedestrians walking in either direction, and bullock carts filled with produce and goods were moving along slowly. Some young men whizzed by in chariots pulled by pairs of horses.

Chandragupta said, gesturing towards the road, 'You know, the Uttarapath runs right until Rajgriha, the Nanda king's capital.'

Rohan asked, 'Is this Takshashila?'

'Yes, we've reached.' Chandragupta said cheerily. 'We'll soon reach the city gates.'

In a few minutes, the group approached tall wooden walls made of gigantic tree trunks embedded in a row as far as the eye could see. Soldiers were marching up and down the wide ramparts. Every few hundred metres, there were guard towers. A wide moat filled with lotuses and water lilies surrounded them. The flowers filled the air with a lovely scent. Ducks and ducklings glided across the moat's waters. The Himalayas rose up faintly in the far distance.

They walked up to a very large wooden gate that was open. Though the guards posted here weren't questioning travellers, they were keeping a keen eye on the comings and goings of all.

Once inside the walled city, Chandragupta said, 'It's almost dark. Come, let's go straight to the Acharya's house – it's right here. I'm sure the Acharya will let you stay the night.'

The others weren't at all sure that they wanted to meet Chanakya, who sounded very, very intimidating.

'Oh, my fellow students will be there too,' added Chandragupta as an afterthought.

The group halted outside a large, sprawling cottage with a wooden fence around it. It was a low, single-storey house made of beaten mud with a raised, covered platform in the front. The roof was covered with rust-coloured earthen tiles. The outside walls were plastered with lime and had a few narrow windows covered with wooden lattices.

A man rushed out of the house. He was of medium height and build and had a deeply pockmarked face. His thick and fleshy lips were pressed together sternly. He was dressed in a yellow dhoti, and his upper body was covered with a cloth that went across his chest diagonally. His head was fully-shaven except for a patch on the back – much like that of the Hindu priests the kids had seen

before. But unlike their tidy *shikha*s, this man's patch of hair was long and open, and swung wildly across his back as he strode up. He had deep frown lines between eyes that appeared cold.

He was glaring at them ferociously.

• • • • • • • • • • • • •

9

Ansh gulped nervously while Elfu tried to hide behind Rohan. The Brahmin stared at them a few moments longer, before shifting his gaze to Chandragupta.

'Ah, you are back, my lad,' his face breaking into an unexpected smile. 'I hoped you would be back earlier.' His face turned solemn. 'I have already heard…King Puru came off the worse, but he and Alakshendra have formed a treaty. This is most grave news for Bharat…'

'Acharya!' Chandragupta exclaimed with a smile. He went over and reverently touched his guru's feet. 'Yes,' he said, 'I must tell you all about it – I was right there, in the thick of things, but first, please meet my friends from the south. They have been on a long journey. This is…err…' He was pointing to Rohan when the kids realized they had somehow not told Chandragupta their names yet.

Their modern names were hardly going to do. They were in a soup now!

Suddenly, Rohan remembered a TV serial he'd watched on Indian mythology and had a flash of inspiration.

'Err…I'm Rohaniputra. This is Anshaputra, this is Noorputra, and this is…' he gave a panicked glance to Zoya. They didn't even have the letter Z in ancient India!

She stepped in smoothly, 'I am Jambuputra.'

Chanakya gave them an incredulous look. 'Son of a *jamun*? That's a strange name. Your names are most... unusual, most curious indeed!'

Oops! thought Zoya. She blurted, 'Well, in the south, far away, far, far away, where we are from, you know...we had an ancestor who loved eating *jamun*s...I mean *jambu*s... Uh...so, my parents named me in his honour.'

'Hmm,' replied Chanakya with a piercing look. Zoya felt he could see right through her lies.

He turned to Chandragupta and said shortly, 'They can sleep on the veranda tonight. Eat and get to bed. Tomorrow, I want every detail of what you witnessed.' Chanakya stalked off with a flourish.

Chandragupta turned to them with a smile and said, 'Don't worry, Acharya's bark is worse than his bite... usually! Come on.'

They first led Elfu to the back where some humped white cows were grazing lazily on hay. 'Your *gaja* can stay here. He'll be quite safe,' said Chandragupta.

Elfu looked disdainfully at the grass and hay laid out for the animals' dinner and tried to follow the kids back, but Rohan sternly told him to stay. He turned his back to them with a pained harrumph, dropping some steaming elephant dung to make his displeasure quite clear. At the pungent smell, the kids scurried off.

• • • • • • • • • • • • • •

Around the corner, they saw a busy scene. Boys of various ages were bustling around. All had shaven heads, save the *shikha*, and were wearing simple cotton dhotis. They gave the newcomers quizzical looks, but didn't say anything.

Zoya pointed to a corner with a U-shaped mud stove and a large earthen *ghada* bubbling on top of it and exclaimed, 'Look! That *chulha* is exactly like the ones I have seen in villages – my mom makes me go all the time to visit rural artisans with her.' She rolled her eyes.

The familiar aroma of lentils, rice, ginger and turmeric all cooking together rose from the pot.

Ansh went up and peered inside the vessel, his face turning sour. 'I can't get away from khichri even 2,000 years in the past,' he muttered in disgust.

Zoya, though, inhaled deeply and exclaimed, 'It smells delicious!' Even Noor and Rohan gazed at the pot longingly. They had survived an entire day on dry *chana*. Even grass would taste amazing at this point.

Chanakya's students sat down on the floor. Chandragupta led the others up to them and gestured that they should sit as well. As the four settled into a cross-legged position, the students all recited a short Sanskrit mantra in unison.

Brahmaarpanam brahma havih, brahmaagnau brahmanaa
hutam |
Brahmaiva tena gantavyam, brahma-karma-samaadhinaa ||

The act of offering is Brahman, the oblation is Brahman,
the instrument of offering is Brahman, and the fire into
which the offering is made is also Brahman. For one who
is thus absorbed in the actions of Brahman, he alone
reaches Brahman.

After the recitation, everyone poured some water on the ground next to them. The children looked on, a little bewildered, before trying to copy their actions.

Everyone began digging heartily into the khichri served on banana leaves, glugging down salted buttermilk in large terracotta tumblers. The kids demolished the steaming hot food in no time, even Ansh.

As soon as their heads touched the grass mats laid out on the veranda, they were out for the count.

• • • • • • • • • • • • •

Rohan was the first to wake the next morning. It was barely dawn. His eyes still closed and mind wandering, he lay listening to the chirps and cheeps of hundreds of birds all around him. He came to when he heard a particularly raucous, loud squawk. It was not musical in the least.

A peacock was standing close to him, its feathers on full display as it strutted about. Its female companions were ignoring him, looking distinctly unimpressed. *Man, I was born two thousand years too late*, Rohan thought wistfully to himself. *Ancient India was a nature lover's paradise, with millions of birds and animals.*

Chandragupta came up to them and said sunnily, 'Rise and shine! Come on, up you get!'

The children sat up sleepily, watching the students walking out of the cottage in a single file. 'Where's everyone heading?' asked Noor. 'It's barely dawn...'

'Why, for our morning bath, silly!' replied Chandragupta. 'And the daily sun worship. No breakfast until we do!'

'Ahh,' said Zoya, perking up at the thought of brekkie. 'What're we waiting for, then?'

Soon, they were at a small river with a slushy bank. Some of the other students casually flung off all their clothes and waded in. Cupping water in their palms, they held it up to the sun and chanted: '*Om bhur bhuvah swaha, tatsavitur varenyam...*'

Ansh said excitedly, 'Wait, that's the Gayatri Mantra! My mother recites it all the time!'

Rohan gave him a warning look as Chandragupta exclaimed in great surprise, 'But women never chant this sacred mantra...'

Oh man, they were falling into one trap after another, thought Ansh glumly.

Zoya ventured timidly, 'Well...you know things are a bit different...in our village...in the south.' Even as she said this, she thought the situation was getting ridiculous.

Chandragupta looked at them intensely and said, 'This Dakshin Bharat seems to be on another planet instead of another region!' He added, 'Well, what are you waiting for? Undress and let's go!'

Zoya blushed bright red and gave Noor an agonized look. How on earth were they going to get out of this one? Was their game finally up?

• • • • • • • • • • • •

10

Noor went and jumped into the river with all her clothes on. Zoya followed her swiftly.

'What on earth are you doing?' asked Chandragupta in astonishment.

'Well, back home in our village in the south, it's customary to bathe like this. Isn't it, Ro and Ansh?' said Noor.

'Right, yes!' The boys caught on and followed them quickly into the river with their clothes on.

Chandragupta looked on, bemused. He really had to visit the south soon. What a place!

Soon they were walking back, four of them in dripping wet clothes. Ah, well. It was hot – they'd soon dry off. They passed other students trooping back in twos and threes, giving them slightly curious looks.

Once they were back, Chandragupta went inside the house. Turning his back on the others, Ansh checked his phone anxiously for the twentieth time. His ma was going to be climbing the walls with fear soon. He'd never been away from her for so long.

Suddenly, there was a change in the elephant app that had landed them in trouble in the first place. A large home button appeared. Ansh pressed it and shouted, 'Guys! There's a message!' They all huddled around his phone and read: 'For Home Journey. Go to the Banyan Tree. Outside Takshashila Palace. At Dusk.'

They turned to each other with grins of pure relief. 'I think we might just make it back,' said Rohan.

'If we get through today...' added Ansh glumly.

A little later, as they sat with the other students and gulped big tumblers of creamy cow milk and the most delicious bananas for breakfast, Chandragupta turned to them and said, 'Why don't you come along with me today? You can see how we do things in Takshashila.'

A shadow fell across them. They looked up to see the scowling figure of Chanakya looming directly above.

'Young Chandragupta, I want to see you at the earliest,' He walked off.

Zoya asked Chandragupta tentatively, 'Could we come and listen?' She just had to see Chandragupta and Chanakya interacting with each other for herself.

'Why not?' replied Chandragupta after a moment's pause. 'I don't think Acharya should object...' he said a little dubiously. 'Let's try...'

Chattering away, the children followed him into the yard with a large banyan tree that provided some shade against the blazing summer sun. Chanakya sat cross-legged with his eyes closed, his back completely straight. He paid no heed to them but chanted aloud 'A man learns only by listening. A man loses his stupidity only by listening. A man reaches salvation only by listening.' He opened his eyes and stared at the four children meaningfully.

'Ouch,' muttered Rohan. 'I think that was meant for us.'

They fell completely silent. Chanakya seemed to have that effect on people.

'So? Tell me everything,' said the guru, turning to his favourite student.

Chandragupta replied, 'Acharya, King Puru fought bravely, very bravely indeed. But that Yavana devil is too wily for words. He didn't even wait for the rains to pass before attacking – have you ever heard of something like that? Doesn't he know that no one ever fights during the monsoon months? He somehow found a shallow ford and sneaked across the overflowing river at night, completely ambushing King Puru's forces. Oh, and what ingenious battle formations! And those long, deadly spears don't let the enemy anywhere close to his soldiers. They are so heavy! I have no idea how they are so skilled at using them.'

'Hmm, discipline and practice,' answered Chanakya briefly.

Chandragupta burst out, 'But what a schemer that Alakshendra is! He extended his hand in friendship to King Puru. Now they are going to conquer the rest of Bharat together, and I don't know what we can do to stop them!' He looked dejected.

Zoya spoke up hesitantly.

'I think if Alexander's soldiers had the least idea of what awaits them as they go further east, they would run back to Greece straight away! Isn't the Nanda king's army ten times the size of Porus's army? They don't know, do they? So…what if they somehow heard about it?'

Chanakya looked at her with a thoughtful expression before gazing out into the distance for a few moments. 'Ahh,' he muttered determinedly, 'I have it. I know what to do now to save Bharat.' Chanakya closed his eyes as though meditating and would not be drawn into explaining his strategy. He kept repeating, 'What your mind thinks should not come to your lips. Protect your secret at all costs. Only then will you win.'

Everyone looked on inquisitively. As Zoya's curiosity got the best of her, she entreated the Acharya once more to tell them his plan.

Chanakya looked at Zoya and intoned, 'Don't be too straight in life. For the straightest trees are the first to be cut down, while the twisted ones survive the longest.' She gazed at him, baffled as ever.

Meanwhile, a fierce-looking man entered the yard and came up to Chandragupta. 'Time for your weapons lesson, young man.'

Chandragupta jumped up and said, 'My favourite part of the day! Come and watch, friends!'

As they walked to an adjoining open field, the young lad told the children, 'The morning is all about battles and war.'

Noor was excited. She loved martial arts and had been learning karate for years.

'Oh, what all do you have to do, Chandu?' she asked.

'Well, everything to do with the art of war, really. The master trains me physically and teaches me how to wield different weapons. I also practise how to control horses and elephants. Some days we study details of how to make

the best use of each of the four army divisions – infantry, elephants, chariots and cavalry. Also, when to use different battle formations, that sort of thing.'

Soon, the four children were watching Chandragupta duel with another student.

The pleasant, harmless-looking lad was gone. In his place was a single-minded warrior, parrying and thrusting his deadly sword with complete focus at his opponent. Suddenly, Chandragupta leapt up with one foot extended. He used it to bounce off a nearby tree trunk and landed on top of his friend, his sword held at the boy's neck.

Ansh noted that the steel of the sword had beautiful flowy markings, like a watercolour painting. He'd never seen anything like it.

'Do you yield?' demanded Chandragupta, breathing hard.

'Yes, yes – get off me, Chandra!' said the other boy, completely winded. 'Why do you take everything so seriously? It's just a class, you know!'

Chandragupta replied earnestly, 'As Acharya says, whether it's something big or small, whatever you do, you must do it with all your might.'

His friend snorted and replied laughingly, 'Well, you're the only one who takes his sayings to heart so conscientiously. That explains why you are his favourite... Come on, let's go for archery.'

Later, as they were eating a simple lunch of rice and curd – much to Ansh's dismay – Chandragupta explained his daily schedule to them. 'Acharya makes me work from morning to evening. It's really exhausting. He is writing a book on government, called the *Arthashastra*, which explains how princes should be educated. He absolutely insists on trying out all his theories on me!'

Zoya's eyes widened at this casual remark. *I am present at a time in history when the legendary Arthashastra is still being finalized?* she thought. She could hardly believe it. She simply had to get hold of a copy...somehow!

Ansh eagerly broke in, 'By the way, you have such a beautiful sword! What is it made of?'

'Oh, don't you have this in Dakshin Bharat?' asked Chandragupta. 'Well, it's made from a very special local steel – extremely hard and it never, ever rusts. Alakshendra is trying to gather all the steel that he can from Bharat, because it's so much better than anything he has ever seen!'

Chandragupta smiled and carried on, 'My morning routine is just the beginning. After lunch is when my brainpower is pushed to its limit.'

'Wow,' muttered Rohan, 'we only study for the first half of each day...and that feels like a lot!'

Chandragupta replied a little boastfully, 'Well, the Nanda Empire isn't going to conquer itself, is it? I have to take it seriously.'

Zoya smiled and interjected, 'So, what do you have to do after lunch then?'

'I don't know how it is in the south...' he replied with a meaningful look at her, '... but here, we all must learn the four Wings of Knowledge. The first is called *trayi* – it's about understanding and learning the three Vedas and the Upanishads by heart. This teaches us what is right and what's wrong – dharma and *adharma*.

'Then comes *anvikshiki* or what we like to jokingly call Working on Ourselves. That's because we must work and work and work! During *lokayata* lessons, Acharya makes us debate with each other to hone our skills of logic and reasoning – he's not happy unless things get pretty heated up! Then comes philosophy. The session ends with yoga to improve our powers of concentration.'

'Yoga?' cried Ansh. 'We learn it every week. My favourite pose is *shavasana*,' he chortled.

'It would be – the dead-man pose!' retorted Noor. 'I can do a headstand for five whole minutes...should I show you?' She made to get up.

Chandragupta interjected hastily. 'Err...no, no, please finish your food. As you know, once we get up, we can't sit back down to eat until the next meal.'

'Okay, Chandu...if you say so,' Noor replied, settling down sulkily.

Chandragupta continued, 'Anyway, then we...'

'Wait, there's more?' interrupted Rohan. 'I'm getting tired just listening to you!' Rohan's idea of school was biology, geography...and that was about it!

Chandragupta's laugh boomed out. 'There's a lot more!' he said. 'I still haven't told you about *varta* – study of the economy, including agriculture, cattle-rearing, trade, wealth – and *dandaniti* or how to dispense justice. Once all this is done, we get a break of sorts during which we sit in groups and learn our country's history. The Puranas tell us about the good and evil kings of the past, and the Dharmashastras tell us about the rishis and *munis*.'

Everyone's eyes had glazed over at this information overload. Only Zoya still looked bright and curious. She wondered, what history is he talking about? Most of the Indian history we are taught begins now – with the Mauryan dynasty! She giggled silently to herself.

'But that's not all,' Chandragupta continued. 'To become a well-rounded man, we also need to learn the eighteen *shilpa*s, including music, painting, poetry, mathematics, engineering, snake charming, magic, the art of finding treasures… As you can imagine, I am working rather hard on the last one.' He wiggled his eyebrows knowingly.

'Wow!' said Rohan with a wide-eyed look. 'You lot must be at it from morning to night.'

'You must have loads of books about so many subjects – where's your library?' Zoya asked eagerly. 'I would love to see it!'

'Books?' scoffed Chandragupta. 'Are you serious? No way! We wish we could be that lazy. We students must know all the texts by heart. As the Acharya always says, "Knowledge stored only in books and money lent out is never available to you when you need it."'

There was pin-drop silence. All four children sat there, completely gobsmacked, even Zoya. Learn the entire textbook and never write anything down? Study twelve to fourteen hours a day? Live with your teacher and be at his beck and call 24x7? Eat khichri day and night?

Boy, they were glad to be living in modern times. Now if they could only get back there…

• • • • • • • • • • • •

11

After they finished their meal, Chandragupta said, 'Come, let me show you around Takshashila – it's a really special city.'

Rohan interjected, 'Yes, sounds great, but we must take Elfu along. He gets anxious when I am not around.' He hurriedly whispered to the others in English, 'We can try and see how to get to the palace once we are in the centre of town...'

Chandragupta looked a bit doubtful. 'Hmm, an elephant walking around town... It will slow us down considerably.' But seeing Rohan's determined expression, he shrugged and said, 'Okay, okay. Let's take the little *gaja* with us, why not?'

A little after leaving Chanakya's compound, the motley crew reached the city's main road. Soon, they were walking amongst tall multi-storey structures with large verandas. Their windows had wooden lattices in a variety of patterns. A few of the buildings even had cages hanging outside, holding brilliantly coloured birds.

Chandragupta started pointing out different buildings. 'That's the law school,' he said, gesturing to one. 'Don't ever get into an argument with one of the students there – they won't let you get away for a week. Ask me, I know well!

'That over there is the medical school. I've heard some crazy stories about that place! The *vaidya*s there can rebuild a nose and even cut open a woman to take out an unborn child!' He looked horrified as he said this.

'What?' exclaimed Noor loudly. 'That sounds insane! Are you sure, Chandu?' she asked, utterly shocked.

'I promise it is true. Although I agree it sounds mighty strange,' he replied with a chuckle. 'Aah! This here is the prestigious military academy,' Chandragupta stopped in front of a large, grand-looking complex. 'I come here for some of my classes. Princes come from all over the country to study here – from Kosala, Magadha, Kashi...' he added proudly.

Then he scowled ferociously. 'Though if I ever happen to come across that Nanda king's brat, I will tear him apart with my own hands.' In that moment, the children got a glimpse of the grim warrior king he would become, and shivered.

The city was crowded, and they saw throngs of people from all walks of life – young students returning from their classes, women going to the market, men going about their business. Most were dressed in cotton robes so blindingly white that they seemed to have been washed with some special detergent.

'Hey!' shouted Ansh, pointing ahead. 'What on earth is happening here?'

Chandragupta and the others looked in the direction Ansh was indicating and saw a group of men who looked like they were dressed for a fancy-dress party. Though all the men wore full-length robes in white, their long beards were dyed in different colours. One beard was bright red while another was blue. There were yet others that were green and purple. The men held old-fashioned umbrellas to shade themselves from the scorching sun. They walked most peculiarly, taking short steps, mincing along slowly.

'Look at their shoes!' exclaimed Zoya. The men wore white-leather, high-heeled *chappals* with multicoloured soles.

Rohan grinned and said, 'Well, well, their own little rainbow parade!'

As they continued to look, they saw a few more similarly dressed men in the distance.

Seeing their astonishment, Chandragupta said, 'Many trendy gentlemen from the well-to-do families of Takshashila dress like this. Is it not so in Dakshin Bharat?'

'No!' exclaimed Rohan forcefully, 'Absolutely not. We dress plainly. Very, very plainly.'

'Err, but this is so much more interesting,' added Ansh weakly. By this time, they were passing another large complex of buildings. Pointing to a spacious-looking building, Chandragupta said, 'Ah. This is the academy for girls. Some of the students here are sent from far-off cities by their parents, imagine that?'

'Wait!' shouted Noor. 'Girls are allowed to be educated in Takshashila?'

'Well, yes, but it's still quite rare and the subjects are far fewer,' replied Chandragupta.

'Ah,' said Noor meaningfully, glaring at Rohan. 'So, if I were a girl, I could openly study in Takshashila, hmm?' She whispered to him, 'See! You didn't need to pretend we were boys!' He shrugged.

There was a commotion nearby as a few local soldiers started hastily clearing a path for a procession.

'Oh, yes!' said Chandragupta. 'I almost forgot. King Shobhit is supposed to be meeting with King Ambhi today. King Shobhit is really something else.'

Chuckling mysteriously, he added, 'I guarantee you will not have seen a sight like this in your whole lives!'

The children looked on curiously as the king's attendants walked by, their eyes straight ahead. They were holding silver vessels from which richly scented smoke was escaping.

'Achoo!' sneezed Ansh, his eyes starting to water heavily. 'What is that smell? It's so strong! I think I'm allergic to... Achoo!'

One of the attendants turned and glared at Ansh.

'Be quiet, lad, if you know what's good for you,' the man whispered menacingly. Ansh immediately fell silent – he didn't want to upset anyone of them. Who knew what they would do to him.

Once the attendants had passed, a gilded open palanquin, carried laboriously by eight hefty men, came into view. Luminous pearls dangled from the palanquin's poles and sides. A tall and extremely handsome man sat reclined on it. His fine muslin *dhoti* was heavily embroidered in gold and purple. Clearly, he was this King Shobhit.

Noor whispered piercingly from the side of her mouth. 'It looks so scratchy!' Zoya shushed her warningly, looking at the procession in wonder.

The king was clearly trying his best to look royal, a task made hard as he was practically dripping in jewels in the harsh sun. His arms and wrists were covered in pearls,

and his dangly earrings were set with huge sapphires. He held a sceptre made of pure gold, set intricately with beryl gemstones.

He tried to nod graciously at the crowd gawping at him, but every time he did this, his earrings struck his neck with some force. Eventually, he gave up with a sigh and just looked straight ahead.

Noor whispered again, 'Oh gosh! Just look at his sandals.'

The king's footwear was indeed something to behold. Made of gold-embroidered leather, it was studded with rubies and emeralds and sapphires.

Marching soldiers and bodyguards followed the king's palanquin. Some of them were carrying large tree branches with colourful little birds perched on them. As the spectators looked on, the birds broke into a synchronized song for a few seconds. They repeated this trick every couple of minutes.

Then, Zoya said, 'Guys, look! Am I imagining this? An army of big, burly dogs was marching past now. One soldier was leading five dogs in a row. The scary mastiffs looked neither left nor right and marched ahead with their noses up in the air.

Rohan whispered in disbelief, 'Are we getting pranked? Is this really happening?'

Ansh said, 'There are 150 dogs – I just counted.'

Chandragupta gave a shout of laughter. 'Oh, King Shobhit must be gifting these to Alakshendra,' he said. 'Our dogs are famous all over the world, you know. Even the Persians love them. This isn't even the half of it. King

Shobhit's kingdom has the weirdest way of choosing their king – there is a contest every few years.'

'Aha! A fight to the death!' exclaimed Noor, wildly brandishing an imaginary sword.

'Hardly,' Chandragupta replied scornfully. 'They choose...' he lowered his voice and rolled his eyes as if he could hardly believe what he was going to say, 'the most... *handsome* man to be king.'

As the others looked on at him in disbelief, he added with a scoff, 'Little wonder that they didn't even pretend to fight Alakshendra when he came knocking at their door!'

'What is he doing here, though?' asked Zoya a little impatiently.

Chandragupta replied in hushed tones. 'I have heard he was summoned here after his surrender. He's probably here with gifts to submit to that Yavana. I've heard that Alakshendra plans to celebrate his victory by holding an athletic competition,' Chandragupta added, shaking his head in disapproval.

Noor asked interestedly 'Oh yes? What sort of competition?'

'Umm, I think there will be events like races and boxing and chariot-racing and wrestling...who knows?' said the youth with a dismissive shrug. 'The Yavanas are sports-mad you know. They love nothing better than running themselves into the ground in the name of sportsmanship.'

• • • • • • • • • • • • •

They continued to wander about the bustling streets, gazing at the houses with interest. They passed a street hawker holding a cane basket lined with leaves. 'Come and get your *vattakas*!' he called out repetitively. 'Three for the price of two. Come, get them! Freshly fried, hot *vattakas*!'

Ansh eyed them wistfully...they looked like the delicious deep-fried *vadas* that he hardly ever got to eat.

Suddenly, they heard the loud clanking of cymbals. Noor rushed ahead but then stopped dead in her tracks. She turned around to the group and said faintly, 'Now I've really seen everything...'

The others rushed up to her and were equally gobsmacked at the sight in front of them. In an open square was a circle of dancing elephants! Another elephant stood to one side of the circle with a cymbal fastened to each foreleg.

It used a third cymbal attached to its trunk to rhythmically beat the other two in turn. The dancing

elephants were raising and bending their forelegs as they moved along in rhythm. A drummer and a few mahouts stood by, encouraging them. The children gawked at the crazy scene.

Rohan exclaimed, 'Oh my! Look at Elfu!'

An excited Elfu had nudged his way into the circle and was trying to imitate the other elephants. The children started giggling.

The mahouts came up and addressed Chandragupta. 'This is such a charming little elephant! We must have him for our dancing troupe. How much will you sell him for?'

Rohan looked at them, stupefied.

'We won't take no for an answer,' they said.

•••••••••••••

12

'No!' said Chandragupta. 'Our elephant is a part of our family. We can't give him away for all the riches in the world.'

As the mahouts continued to insist, the children backed away hastily, Rohan pulling a reluctant Elfu by his trunk.

Having got the mahouts off his back, Chandragupta joined them after a few minutes.

As they were walking back towards the market, they came across two Greek soldiers accompanying an intellectual-looking Greek man.

'Why is he wearing a bedsheet?' asked Ansh curiously.

Zoya gave him a concerned, slightly superior look, and said, 'You do know that's the Greek ancestor of a Roman toga, right? I think it's called a himation.'

The Greek soldiers called out to Chandragupta. 'Oi! Sandrokottus! Where have you been? Haven't seen you in a while. Normally, we can't beat you away from the barracks with a stick,' they said with a smirk.

'He, he,' Chandragupta smiled sheepishly. 'I went to see the battle. You lot came off all right!'

'Of course,' said the other soldier pompously. 'Our Macedonian army is the greatest in the world! We've never lost a battle in the last fifteen years.' He puffed up with pride as he said this.

Then, he turned to the man in the Greek robe and said, 'Sire, this is young Sandrokottus, a military student here in Takshashila. We've been interacting a lot with our Indian allies over the past few months. This boy here is interested in all things Greek.'

'Well, that's nice.' replied the man distractedly. 'I'm looking for exotic things to send back to my uncle in Macedonia. I've already gathered wool that grows in trees and the honey that grows in reeds.' There was an amazed look in his eyes as he said this.

'Wool that grows in trees? Honey that grows in reeds? What nonsense!' Ansh whispered loudly in English to the rest. 'Has this man completely lost it!'

Rohan muttered under his breath, 'Sweet reeds? What could he be talking about?'

Zoya was already on it. 'Maybe he means wool...on sheep?' she whispered. 'And honey on bees?'

Ansh rolled his eyes.

Not one to let go of a puzzle, Zoya thought hard, frowning

with the effort. 'Wool on…oohhhh, he means plants, not trees!' she spoke in excited but low tones. 'Cotton! That's native to India. And honey…reeds… Oh, the Greeks have never seen that before too – you know, sugar cane…'

'OH! YES!' All of a sudden, the man in the himation caught sight of Elfu, who was sniffing around for food as usual. 'I must have that elephant! The one thing my dear uncle absolutely insisted upon was one of these strange creatures. And this one has such an extraordinary star sign on its forehead – just like poor, dear Bucephalus!' He turned to the group eagerly and said, 'You must sell him to me! How much is he for? I must have him!'

The children grew alarmed, and Elfu retreated behind Rohan. Did everyone in this world want Elfu?

'No, No!' shouted Rohan. 'He's like my brother. He is not for sale.'

Just as the Greek man opened his mouth to argue, his attention was diverted by a group of stern-looking Indian monks walking by. The monks were properly naked. The kids blushed hotly and tried looking anywhere else but at them.

'Ahh!' shouted the Greek man excitedly. 'Are you gymnosophists? I must take you back as well. Uncle was most curious to meet members of your religion.'

The oldest among them said sternly, 'I am Dandamis, a Jain monk. These are my pupils. And who might you be?'

The Greek replied haughtily, 'I am Callisthenes – nephew of the most famous philosopher in the known world – the great Aristotle himself. I demand you join us.

Our great leader Alexander commands it. He is the son of God, you know. Don't make us force you.'

Dandamis gave him a terrible look and spat out angrily. 'Tell your great leader, if he is the son of God, then so am I!'

'I want nothing from him or you, for what I have is enough,' continued the monk. 'All your worldwide wandering over land and sea is utterly useless. You lot are nothing but a nuisance to yourselves and others. You have nothing I desire. This land is enough for me while I live; and when I die, I shall finally be rid of my poor body and be free.'

The Greek philosopher backed away hastily, muttering, 'Let Lord Alexander deal with this man himself.' He glared at the children and stalked off, saying, 'But I'll have that elephant, mark my words!'

The children looked admiringly at Dandamis, not least because he had saved Elfu. They couldn't have faced down those scary Greeks like he had. However, the old man looked neither left nor right as he walked away majestically, followed by his disciples.

'Phew!' Chandragupta exhaled with relief. 'That was lucky. Acharya Dandamis is so strict that no one messes with him. Your *gaja* sure is in demand, eh?' He patted Elfu's trunk gently and the elephant immediately draped his trunk around Chandragupta's neck blissfully.

He added, 'Come, there's someone I want you to meet. He is the most famous doctor throughout the sixteen *mahajanapadas*. For the last few years, he has been writing the thickest book on Ayurveda – the science of life. I have to deliver the Acharya's message to him.'

Chandragupta turned off the main road and onto a narrower side road lined with houses. A few metres in, he turned again, into a smaller road parallel to the main road they had been on.

After walking for a few minutes, Chandragupta stopped before a large house similar to Chanakya's. In the front yard, an old, white-haired rishi in a simple white *dhoti* was sitting with a large group of male students, dressed in cotton dhotis. Nearby, a pan sizzled over a small open fire. Something was cooking – it smelled like eggs.

'That smells yum – I am so hungry,' lamented Zoya.

The rishi looked up as the group approached. Smiling, he said, 'Ah, young Chandragupta! Come, try this herbal recipe I've been experimenting with. It's meant to make young ones like you strong and vigorous.'

Chandragupta bent down and touched his feet. Smiling ruefully he said, 'Acharya Charaka, I am always wary of your new recipes... and what you put in them!'

Laughing, Charaka gestured to a student, who served the guests bite-sized portions of omelette.

Zoya took a large bite and was savouring the taste when the guru said, 'This is a crocodile-egg omelette, mixed with rice flour and cooked in pure ghee – strong enough to boost the vitality of even the dead!'

Zoya almost gagged in shock. Crocodile egg! Gross! she thought, hastily swallowing the food in her mouth without tasting it further. The other children looked appalled and refrained from touching their portions, no matter how hungry they were.

Chandragupta saw their faces and started shaking with laughter. 'These are my friends, Acharya Charaka,' he said. 'They are from Dakshin Bharat and not used to your special dishes!'

Charaka chortled before smiling at them kindly. 'Okay, try this one instead. A spoon a day keeps the doctor away!'

As they went up reluctantly to take a spoonful each, Ansh ate his and exclaimed loudly, 'Oh, its *chyawanprash*. Yurgh! My mum makes me eat it every day.'

Charaka stared at him, astonished. 'How do you know what this is? I developed the recipe only earlier this year.'

• • • • • • • • • • • • • •

13

Ansh looked horrified. His eyes opened wide, and he started stammering.

Noor rushed to his rescue. 'Err, Acharya Charaka, you are so famous in the south! All the news about you is brought to us by travellers and pilgrims, you know.'

Charaka looked pleased, but still puzzled.

The children made a hurried exit as soon as they could and headed back to the town centre. The way things were going, it would be a miracle if they finally managed to escape undiscovered.

After walking a few yards, Chandragupta turned to them and said, 'I need to head to the outskirts for another errand...so...'

It was time to say goodbye. It was soon going to be dusk, and they needed to reach the palace.

Zoya cleared her throat and said, 'Yeah, we too have to visit an old friend of our father's. He lives near the palace. So...we'll catch up afterwards?'

Chandragupta said, 'Of course! We must do that. Why don't you come back to Acharya Chanakya's later? Just ask anyone for directions if you get lost – they all know his place.'

After a cheerful 'see you', the youth had turned to walk away when he felt multiple arms flinging themselves at him from behind.

Astonished, Chandragupta turned around and saw Noor and Ansh hugging him fiercely.

'I'll miss you, Chandu...' Noor muttered.

'You've been so great!' added Ansh.

Even Rohan looked misty-eyed as he said goodbye.

'I know you will be a great conqueror one day!' Zoya whispered in Chandragupta's ear. 'Never doubt yourself,'

Chandragupta gave them all a concerned look. 'I'll see you soon. Take care. And Takshashila is not as scary as you seem to think... See you later!' He pushed them aside gently and walked away, turning back to look at them thoughtfully.

'We'll never see him again... I'm so sad!' mourned Zoya.

'But also excited 'cause we're goin' home!' chimed in Ansh.

'Right,' said Rohan, coming back to reality with a start. 'Let's hurry. It's almost dusk!'

Up ahead, they could see the large wooden palace towering over the landscape. There were gilded pillars all around it – columns covered in gold-embossed vines with silver birds interspersed throughout. The overall effect was bedazzling.

The group was making its way to the palace when Zoya wondered aloud, 'Where's this large banyan tree, then?'

The children looked around anxiously. After a few moments, they spotted a gigantic banyan tree, off to one side, in the distance. They hurriedly strode up to it, worried it might be too late.

As they walked around the tree's huge trunk, Rohan exclaimed, 'Look, a star mark! This must be it!' There was a peculiar star-shaped gnarly knot on the tree trunk.

'All right, everyone, switch on your phones.' said Zoya. As their mobiles powered on, their screens turned an eerie blue once again and the elephant icon came up.

Ansh pressed the 'Home' button impatiently, wanting to be back in his room already. Text prompts appeared on their phone screens: Touch. The. Star. And. Chant: *Mahagaja, Mahagaja, Mahagaja.* Do. It. Before. Dark.'

By now, the sun had dipped right down.

'Hurry, everyone,' said Zoya. They all touched the knot in the tree. As they began chanting the mantra awkwardly, Rohan suddenly realized that Elfu's trunk was no longer in his hand! He looked up in panic and saw that a band of Greek soldiers had surrounded the little elephant, their long spears pointing at him threateningly, while he gazed at Rohan imploringly.

'Elfuuuuuu!' screamed Rohan. 'Get back here, quick!'

But it was too late. The world started spinning faster and faster. Lights started flashing and the sound of the wind boomed in their ears.

Once again, everything was still.

• • • • • • • • • • • • • •

14

When they opened their eyes, the children were back at the cave. Ansh looked very relieved. He checked his phone and exclaimed, 'Hey! You won't believe this! No time has passed since we left. It's still Saturday lunchtime! My mom won't even know I was gone.'

Noor started skipping with glee. 'We had an adventure! I still can't believe it. But why us? Why did it happen to us?' She cast a glance at Rohan, who was sitting in despair on the floor, his head in his hands, tears starting to fill his eyes. 'Oh, Rohan! I'm so sorry about Elfu.'

Zoya looked at them and took out her phone without a word. A blue light filled the cave as she started tapping urgently. She squealed, 'Look! There's an elephant-shaped button!' As she pressed it, a revolving circle appeared on the screen and the text 'Locating elephant' flashed in the centre.

They all watched with bated breath as the circle stopped revolving and the text changed to: '*Elephant located. 326 BCE.*'

Rohan switched on his phone and Elfu's location flashed on it as well. He stood up with purposeful energy, a determined look on his face. 'Look, I must go back for Elfu,' he said resolutely. 'You all carry on to the resort.'

Ansh looked anxiously at the mouth of the cave. He was so not ready to go back on this crazy time-travel ride! He'd had enough. He had no idea how and why they had landed so long ago in the past, and he didn't want to know either! He took a few steps towards the exit, but then he stopped. 'No!' he exclaimed. 'All for one and one for all! Even if it's to do with that pesky elephant.'

He grinned and put his fist out. Zoya and Noor came up and did the same, crying, 'Yes! All for one and one for all! We'll figure out the rest later...'

Now Rohan really looked like he was going to cry. He came up and gave them a bearhug. 'Thanks, you guys! This means everything.'

All of them held hands as Rohan pressed the button. After the whooshing and whistling and flashing, when the children opened their eyes, they realized they were on the banks of a river again. But it was not the Jhelum, which they had crossed before with Chandragupta. This river was narrower, its flow less intense. The landscape looked different too. There were many more open fields, and fewer trees and, thankfully, no dead bodies. The ground was slushy and muddy. Thick, dark monsoon clouds were gathering in the sky, hiding the sun.

In the distance, they saw a military camp.

'Come,' whispered Rohan, 'let's see what is happening – Elfu must be here somewhere!'

As they crept up, fat droplets began to plop down. They saw bands of Greek soldiers looking grim and muttering dourly to one another.

'Wow, they do not look happy,' exclaimed Zoya.

'How do we get inside this camp, though?' wondered Rohan, looking around for a way in.

'I know!' said Noor, confidently. 'Let's rush at the guards and take their swords!'

The other three gave her withering looks. 'Yes, Ms Rani of Jhansi – such a well-thought-out plan,' scoffed Ansh.

'Okay, okay, don't squabble,' said Zoya. 'Let's walk around and see if one of the other entry points is less guarded.'

As they skirted around the camp, they realized that one gate was a trade entrance of sorts. Many local people and carts carrying all sorts of supplies for the camp – heaps of fruits and vegetables, barrels of oil, mounds of wheat and rice – were coming and going through this gate.

'Bingo!' whispered Rohan exultantly. 'We'll have to pretend to be tradesmen.'

They crept closer and saw a driverless cart stacked with bales of hay. They each grabbed one and covered their faces almost entirely.

Rohan strode up to the gate and muttered in a fake deep voice, 'Delivery for the great general's horses.'

They were ushered through without a squeak. They proceeded smoothly until they found themselves close to a large, grand tent, guarded by soldiers. Outside the entrance, a large group of Greek soldiers was gathered, dressed most strangely. The plain fabric of their frock-like uniforms seemed to have been replaced with cotton fabric in all sorts of colourful prints.

Ansh exclaimed, 'This feels like a Fabindia store! My mom loves shopping from there.'

Some of the soldiers were sitting on the muddy ground, clutching their heads and weeping. A few others were pleading loudly.

'Oh, Great One! Listen to us. Oh, listen to us! How long must we wander about the world?! Our hair is turning grey, and our children must be grown by now.'

The whole group began chanting, 'We want to go home! We want to go home!'

Ansh thought to himself – me too!

One soldier came forward and held up his hand in front of the rest, gesturing for them to stop speaking. Then, he went a bit closer to the entrance of the tent and exclaimed loudly in pathetic tones, 'Come and look at us, O Alexander. Just look at us!' He clutched his blue and yellow flower-patterned tunic despairingly. 'Even our clothes from home have disintegrated in this never-ending rain. It hasn't stopped for seventy days! Seventy days! We are reduced to wearing…these…Indian…' his voice trailed off in utter loathing.

Another soldier chimed in, holding out red, bumpy arms, 'We can defeat any enemy for you…but not the mosquitoes here!'

The children looked at each other. Rohan gestured to them, and they quietly crept around to the back of the tent.

From inside the tent came loud shouting. 'This is ridiculous! They've been at it like this for three days! I'll execute every last one of them. I just want to carry on!'

Zoya whispered, 'That sounds like…'

'…Alexander himself!' finished Noor.

Ansh spotted a hole near the base of the tent and immediately knelt to peer through it. Soon, the others were jostling for a look too.

Alexander was fuming and red in the face, looking as if he was about to have an apoplectic fit. He was growling at three of his generals. 'Why can't we go on? Just a few miles across the River Hyphasis is the end of the world. Everyone knows the world ends after India. I want to see the end of the world!' he shouted, stomping his feet.

His favourite dog Peritas started howling in sync with his beloved master's ranting.

Bewildered, the children looked at one another and shrugged.

One of the generals said, 'O Great Leader, if we don't heed our men now, I fear there will be a widespread revolt. They have followed you faithfully for the last ten years. Don't put them to another impossible test now. Their patience wears thin.'

Another general added, 'The soldiers are miserable here and absolutely spooked by the rumours. They had such a hard time against Porus when he had only twenty thousand soldiers. All they have been hearing in the last few months is that thousands of soldiers of Dhanananda's army are waiting for them across the river. Not fifty thousand, not seventy thousand, but two hundred thousand! Not to mention the eighty thousand horsemen and eight thousand war chariots and six thousand elephants.

'All nonsense of course,' he said dismissively. 'But nothing seems to dispel this belief – no discussion, no command, no threats. The men are in utter fear of slaughter. They just won't go on. They want to go home now,' added the general.

Alexander flung himself into a chair and brooded intensely. He'd already spent many days arguing with his usually loyal soldiers. This couldn't go on. He was facing an outright rebellion on his hands. Their incessant wailing needed to stop – he couldn't take it any longer.

After a few minutes, Alexander stood up and said decisively, 'Right. Well. No point crying over spilt milk. We can come back next year. Immediately announce the packing up of the camp and prepare the altars. Make sure those large-sized bridles and furniture are finished by then. We will move as soon as the sacrifices are performed tomorrow.'

One of the generals whispered to his friend, 'Ahh, that's more like it. Our leader doesn't waste a minute once he makes up his mind.'

The generals dispersed. Soon, the children could hear sounds of laughter and great rejoicing coming from the front end of the camp. The Greek soldiers were ecstatic that they were finally getting to go home.

Bustling activity began across the encampment. Like an army of organized ants, the Greek soldiers started packing up their camp, and their loot, of course.

Zoya exclaimed, 'Wait! The Greeks are retreating! I can't believe it!'

Rohan said despairingly, 'But where is Elfu?'

The children started walking amidst the tents, looking for their elephant friend. They held on to their bales of hay in case they were questioned and needed an excuse.

The camp was huge and disorganized, and it took time to cover it from one end to the other. The children sneaked past what looked like a haphazardly set up market area, where local Indians were selling their wares, and came up to the enclosures for animals. Elfu, however, was nowhere to be seen. Dispirited, they carried on.

Eventually, they came across a strange sight. A large guarded wooden enclosure was filled with every conceivable type of animal and plant, each kept in separate smaller pens. It was like a Museum of Life, and in a corner enclosure they spotted a woebegone Elfu, looking about disconsolately.

Elfu's merriness seemed to have melted away. A mahout was trying to feed him hay, which he kept pushing away with his trunk.

Rohan collapsed to the ground in profound relief. 'Found him! Phew!'

'But they are going to take him away,' whispered Noor in a panicky voice.

As the others looked around, they saw bullock carts and horses being let into the enclosure. Slowly, they began to be loaded with the different varieties of flora and fauna.

Rohan went straight up to the Yavana guard at the gate of the enclosure. Trying (and failing) to look casual, he asked, 'So, you all are going back home, huh? That's a bit of a surprise… And what's going to happen to this lot, then?' He pointed to the enclosure with the animals and plants.

The guard was in a buoyant mood and extremely chatty. He said, 'I am the luckiest person in the world! I am taking all this back home to Macedonia! Pronto!' he said gesturing behind him. 'The Great Leader is sending them all back as gifts for his teacher, Master Aristotle, who is a most curious man indeed. He's always asking questions until one's head begins to spin round and round!' The soldier laughed loudly at his own words. 'I just can't wait to meet my family. I don't even remember how many years ago I last saw them. I get to leave tomorrow!' He finally ran out of breath and stood there, beaming from ear to ear.

Rohan walked away slowly, in deep despair. *Elfu in Greece? How was he going to stop that from happening?*

• • • • • • • • • • • • • •

The children were sitting on their bales of hay, looking around glumly, trying to come up with ways to rescue Elfu. Suddenly, from the corner of her eye, Zoya noticed something move. As she turned towards it, a disbelieving smile spread across her face.

'Oh. My. God. Everyone, Look!'

• • • • • • • • • • • • •

15

Noor jumped up and rushed over.

'Chandu! How are you?'

Chandragupta's tanned face split into a big, surprised smile. 'Noorputra! Anshaputra! Rohaniputra! Jambuputra! Where have you four been? I got so worried when you didn't turn up that evening at Acharya's. And then to go missing without a trace for so many months without a word...' He looked at them reproachfully.

Oh, thought Zoya, her mind working rapidly. A few months seemed to have passed between their two jumps back in time.

'Err, our father's friend, Shashigupta, took us to Aornos to assist him on an urgent task that same day – we just got back,' said Zoya, trying to explain their absence.

It must have convinced Chandragupta as he was smiling now.

'We left Elfu behind with Uncle Shashigupta's men in Takshashila,' Zoya continued, 'but when we got back, we realized that Elfu had been kidnapped by these awful Greeks!'

'What! *Gaja* is with these Yavana devils? That is most unfortunate...' sympathized Chandragupta. 'I've also been very busy. Acharya is so clever – he had all of us students go around the Yavana camp every day and tell tall tales about the huge armies of the Nandas. It worked beautifully! The soldiers went to Alakshendra and said that they wanted to return home to enjoy their riches. Of course, they won't admit that they are scared. They are pretending they are homesick, but I've heard the whispers!'

Zoya broke in. 'No way! The Greeks are going back because of your rumours?'

Chandragupta smiled and said, 'Well, technically they are Acharya's rumours, and I am helping to spread them, but I'll take the compliment.'

Zoya got a faraway look in her eyes. 'Ingenious. Acharya Chanakya is a genius! That's what he meant...'

Rohan was not the least bit interested in the Greek army or Alexander. He said with urgency, 'Guys, we need to rescue Elfu somehow. He won't be able to survive without me... And I can't imagine my life without him either.' A small tear slid from the corner of his eye and he wiped it away impatiently.

Chandragupta patted Rohan's shoulder sympathetically. 'Wait, I have it! I know how we can rescue *gaja*! We only need a bit of courage and lots of confidence!' He looked at them, very pleased with himself.

'Why don't we put another elephant in *gaja*'s place?'

The children gazed at him admiringly.

Chandragupta stood up swiftly, and said, 'Come on, let's go! I am sure there is an elephant stable here somewhere. No self-respecting king would be without them.' He strode off, beckoning them to follow.

• • • • • • • • • • • •

They could hear the elephants well before they could see them; they could be heard even over the din of the camp. Harrumphs rent the air as the children crept towards the sounds and saw a large elephant stable.

There seemed to be a lot of people around. Chandragupta turned to the others and said, 'I reckon its better we take cover until it gets dark in an hour or so.'

As activity in the camp slowly wound down for the night, Chandragupta led the way to the elephant stable. Once the group let themselves inside the compound, they saw dozens of elephants standing around peacefully.

Suddenly, Chandragupta started making the strangest sounds, deep and basal, almost like they came from the earth itself. The elephants all started swaying as one, extending their trunks towards Chandragupta, as though hypnotized. The youth walked among them, trying to find one that matched Elfu's height. But these were great hulking beasts, chosen to be fearsome fighters, and Elfu was, well, a baby in comparison.

Finally, Chandragupta saw a younger elephant in one corner and said, 'He will have to do.'

He went up to the elephant and whispered something to it in low, guttural tones. The elephant bowed his head before wrapping his trunk affectionately around Chandragupta's waist. The children were stunned. Chandragupta seemed to have a remarkable effect on animals. The elephant was happy to follow the youth like an overgrown puppy who had got its favourite treat.

• • • • • • • • • • • • •

When they got to Elfu's enclosure, they were relieved to see that it was unguarded.

As they entered the gate, Elfu caught scent of Rohan. He started harrumphing at the top of his voice and came gambolling to the edge of the enclosure in utter joy.

'Hush, Elfu. It's okay...' Rohan reached across the makeshift bamboo fence to pet his trunk, trying to quieten him before he gave them away.

Chandragupta quickly drew a star on Fake-Elfu's head with some chalk from his pouch, and they swiftly switched the elephants.

As the children were leading Elfu out, Chandragupta whispered, 'Let me stay with this one until he settles a bit. I'll catch up with you soon.'

Zoya passed by a cart piled with ancient books gathered to send to the great Aristotle. Each book was made of long, thin strips of dried bark, tied together with a string in the middle. There were strange squiggles all over.

Zoya fell behind to gaze at them while the others continued walking. She couldn't believe her eyes – these were actual ancient manuscripts! Looking around to see if anyone was watching, Zoya furtively grabbed a book at random and pushed it swiftly inside her tunic. She knew it was so wrong, but she just couldn't resist. Then she hastened her steps and caught up with the others.

Their hearts in their mouths, the four children and Elfu tried to quietly make their way to the haystacks. They could make up stories about themselves, but how would they explain away an elephant?

They managed to make it without any encounter. As they were covering up Elfu with bales of hay to hide him, Elfu thought it was a game and kept knocking them down. Finally, Rohan had to stand between his legs and hold his trunk down. Soon, Chandragupta joined them and they settled down for the night.

Everyone was relieved to have Elfu back, but there was a snag. Though they kept checking their phones, the app stubbornly remained blank, giving them no clue on how to return home.

Dozens of bonfires glittered across the camp as the Greek soldiers sang happy songs in their own language. They were clearly looking forward to their return home from this insanely hot and wet land.

'Hóson zêis, phaínou
Mēdèn hólōs sù lupoû
Pròs olígon ésti tò zên
Tò télos ho khrónos apaiteî.'

'While you live, shine
Have no grief at all
Life exists only for a short while
And Time demands His due.'

In the background, steady hammering sounds and the sawing of wood could be heard as altars for the sacrifice were erected at super speed.

• • • • • • • • • • • •

The children awoke with a start as loud trumpets were sounded.

A voice boomed in Greek: 'All men gather immediately at the bank of the river for the sacred sacrifice. Take all your belongings. We will soon be on the march. Hey, ho! Hey, ho!'

The children looked at each other. It was time for the final, most dangerous stretch.

• • • • • • • • • • • • •

16

As they had discussed, Rohan and Ansh stayed behind to keep Elfu hidden, while Chandragupta went ahead with the girls. As they made their way to the riverbank, they saw twelve humungous wooden altars, which seemed to touch the sky – each one soaring seventy to eighty feet high. Steps led up to them and huge pyres were burning on top of each. Different symbols were painted onto the wooden pillars holding up each altar.

Noor punched Zoya on her shoulder. 'Look,' she whispered piercingly, pointing to a low wooden platform set a little ahead of the altars. 'That is Fake-Elfu next to the stage.' Fake-Elfu was all dressed up with elaborate face paint and jewellery strung all over him. A merry young animal, he looked about interestedly at all the goings-on.

After a great display of horses and men, Alexander stepped onto the stage with Porus alongside him, with a large group of Greek and Indian soldiers clustered in front on him.

He pronounced grandly 'Even God – me – listens to his devoted men. I have decided we will head back to my capital, Babylon, straight away. I command that this land, as far as the River Hyphasis, is added to the brave King Porus's kingdom, to be ruled in my name.

'Half of you will march with me down the River Indus – we shall conquer all the lands till Babylon! The other half will sail back with Admiral Nearchus.

'This little group,' he gestured in Fake-Elfu's direction, 'will immediately march straight back to Macedonia with these specimens for Master Aristotle! He must be most impatient to start studying them. Let all our countrymen marvel at the many wonders we have seen during our great campaign in India. Men! Be strong and disciplined like the fine Macedonian soldiers you are.'

The drums started beating rhythmically, and the Greek soldiers marched off at a brisk pace, leaving behind the scattered remains of the camp. King Porus's troops started gathering in formation a little distance away.

'What on earth is that?' Zoya pointed to a pile of equipment piled haphazardly on one side.

She walked closer to it and said, 'I think the Greeks have left something behind. Wait. That's surely not meant for a horse, is it? They look like horse bridles and reins – but for a horse that's the size of a full-grown elephant!'

Noor, who had come up next to Zoya, exclaimed, 'And look! These bows and arrows and javelins look like they're meant to be used by giants not humans!' She tried picking up a javelin but was barely able to lift it an inch before staggering under its weight and dropping it.

Chandragupta, Noor and Zoya stood there, looking wide-eyed at the strangely sized arms and riding equipment.

An Indian soldier who was taking a round of the campsite came up to them and laughed scornfully. 'You may very well be amazed. The Great Alakshendra commanded that these oversized things be left scattered all over the camp so people would come and think that the Yavanas were giants and more than human! Huh! Talk about propaganda!'

At this information, Chandragupta rolled his eyes and muttered, 'Wily! I always said so.'

Zoya checked her phone for the hundredth time in frustration. *Were they all doomed to live here forever?* she thought despairingly. Then, suddenly, she saw that the blank screen had changed. It said: '*Altar. Artemis. Star. Go Home. Now.*'

She looked up, and sure enough, each altar had painted symbols indicating some Greek god or the other. Zeus was represented by a great thunderbolt, Apollo with a dazzling sun and wise Athena with an owl. Soon, Zoya saw the altar dedicated to Artemis, the Goddess of the Hunt. Her symbols, a bow, arrow and a moon, were painted on the altar. And right next to the moon was a large five-pointed star.

'Hey, Noor...that's it!' she said urgently. 'Let's get the others and go before someone tears this down and we're stuck here forever!' she whispered to Noor in English so that Chandragupta wouldn't understand.

They made their way back to Rohan and Ansh, who were practically hopping with impatience.

Zoya looked at them meaningfully and turned to Chandragupta, 'You have saved us again, and we are so grateful. But now we must bid farewell to you as we have decided to return to Dakshin Bharat until the situation is a bit more stable here.'

'Oh' said Chandragupta, looking crestfallen, 'I was really looking forward to having you in Takshashila, my brave young friends.'

Elfu gave Chandragupta an affectionate squeeze with his trunk.

'We will see you when we see you, Chandu,' piped in Noor, looking equally sad.

As the children waved goodbye, Chandragupta turned and went off to join King Puru's troops, who were heading back to Takshashila.

As soon as he was out of sight, Zoya said, 'Quick, hurry! There's no time to lose! We must get back to Artemis's altar.'

As they went up to the altar and took out their phones, they heaved a sigh of relief. Almost there.

Just a few seconds more, thought Ansh.

Then, out of nowhere, they heard a loud, angry voice say in Greek, 'Hey, you lot! What are you doing with this elephant?'

Their hearts thumping loudly, all four touched the star together.

This time, Rohan kept a death-grip on poor Elfu's trunk as he jabbed at the button on the app.

As the threatening voice came closer, the wind rushed, and lights flashed like they had before. As they lurched and spun, they knew it was going to be okay.

• • • • • • • • • • • •

17

The children kept their eyes closed until the air around them felt still and calm. They were back in that dank and smelly cave in Goa and could not have been happier!

The four children staggered to the cave's entrance and dragged themselves back to the waterfall. Once they caught sight of the familiar pond, they just collapsed where they stood.

'That was insane!' shouted Noor.

Zoya kept pinching herself. 'We met Chandragupta Maurya, *pinch* and Alexander the Great, *pinch* and Chanakya, *pinch* and Charaka *pinch* – ouch! I pinched myself too hard,' she squealed.

'Well, I am thrilled to be back in my own time and place – can't wait to use my own bathroom again,' said Ansh with a shudder.

Rohan gave him a crooked smile. 'Oh, you know you enjoyed yourself – don't pretend!' He turned to the others and said, 'But seriously, what is that app? How is it connected to Elfu? We have a big mystery to solve!'

Ansh jumped up. 'Later! Let's go, let's go, let's go. Let's go home!' The kids wound their way back slowly, marvelling at all the things that had happened.

As the staff cottages came into view, a thin lady with a dreamy smile and brightly printed flowing dress came up. Ansh ran up to her and hugged her fiercely saying, 'Maa!'

She smiled at them. 'My little rose petals! You are all back so early... Anshu-panshu, you missed me!' she exclaimed with a delighted smile. 'In just three hours?' She touched his forehead to check if he was feverish. 'Did you all enjoy your picnic?'

'Yes, Priya Aunty,' chorused Zoya and Noor.

'How many times have I told you girls to call me Nirvana? None of this "aunty" nonsense. Our souls are all equal in this universe...' she trailed off. 'Oh, I must go prepare for my first Wave Yoga class this evening.'

'Your what?' sputtered Rohan.

'Ah...you must be the new boy. Welcome. I am developing a new type of yoga on the beach, where the poses have to be perfectly in sync with the waves. If not, you'll get washed away! It is great for discipline, I'm finding.' She smiled vaguely into the distance.

Rohan gave the others an incredulous look, at which they shrugged. That was Priya Aunty, sorry – Nirvana, for you.

The children headed to their own family cottages, thankful to be back and still shaking their heads at their unbelievable adventure.

As Zoya unpacked her backpack, she took something out of it with a secret smile.

On her bed lay a sheaf of thin, rectangular sheets, made of some unknown material, bound right in the middle. Funny looking squiggles covered the pages. Zoya immediately googled what script was used in Mauryan times. When the search results showed it was the earliest Brahmi alphabet, she painstakingly compared each squiggly letter and wrote down its English equivalent.

When she was done, Zoya read aloud from her piece of paper: '*Kautilya krit Arthashastra*.'

Zoya sat staring at the manuscript for a while – an original version of Chanakya's *Arthashastra*! She shook her head disbelievingly, before stashing it away in the bottom drawer of her chest.

You never knew what the day was going to bring. Would there ever, ever be another like this one ?

A CONFESSION:
FICTION AND FACTS

⦿ As mentioned in the story, Alexander established the city of Alexandria Bucephalia on the banks of the River Jhelum. Now called Jalalpur Sharif, it lies in Pakistan. Although it is about 220 km from Takshashila, we have reduced the distance to a day's journey in the interests of the story.

⦿ Callisthenes, Aristotle's nephew, accompanied Alexander on his conquests. However, he was executed for speaking up once too often just before Alexander reached Takshashila. We have kept him alive for the sake of our story.

⦿ Charaka is known to have lived in Takshashila. However, there is no certainty about the dates. It is believed he was there sometime between the fifth and third centuries BCE.

⦿ We do not know if any books were sent to Aristotle or whether the Arthashastra had been completed by this time.

⦿ This is an anonymous saying we have quoted:

'Knowledge contained in a book, and money lent
to somebody is never available when you need it.'

⦿ Of course, the plot element that Chanakya deliberately spread the rumours as a piece of misinformation is a figment of our imagination. Roman writers, however, have commented that the Indians may have exaggerated the size of the armies of the Praesii or the eastern kingdom, i.e., Magadha, to discourage the Greeks.

⦿ The royal procession in the text is based on the description by Nearchus, one of Alexander's generals, although the synchronized tweeting of the birds is of our own imagination!

FACT TRACKER
More About the Greeks and the Mauryas

By Buddhist times, around 550 BCE, there were sixteen *mahajanapada*s or 'great countries' in India, extending from the north-west of the subcontinent down to the River Godavari in present-day Andhra Pradesh and Telangana. Andhra Pradesh. All-powerful kings ruled most of these *mahajanapada*s, but some were *gana*s or democracies.

Over time, many were conquered by the kingdom of Magadha, which was ruled by the Nanda dynasty

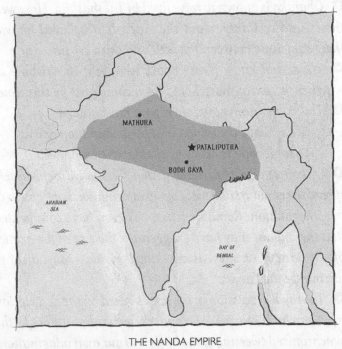

THE NANDA EMPIRE

(around 364 to 324 BCE) when Alexander reached India. The Nandas came to rule a considerable portion of the Indian subcontinent. At Alexander's time, the Nanda king ruling was Dhanananda. He had a reputation for being a cruel ruler, feared and loathed by many. His mighty army, according to the Roman writer Plutarch, had 200,000 foot soldiers, 80,000 horsemen, 8,000 chariots and 6,000 armoured elephants! The Greeks refer to them as Praesii (from *Prachya* or 'easterners') or *Gangaridae* (from the region of the River Ganga).

The Indian north-west (present-day Pakistan), where Alexander first came, was made up of many small kingdoms. The parts west of the River Indus – Gandhara, Kamboja and Sindh – had already been conquered and absorbed by the Persian Empire in the sixth century BCE and paid regular tribute to Persia in gold and soldiers. Tales of India's riches were rife in the western world, which made conquering India very desirable to Alexander. Indian soldiers were part of the Persian forces that attacked Greece in the fifth century BCE.

Indians had contact with ancient Greeks. whom they called 'Yavana', based on what the Persians called them. 'Yavana' was derived from the word 'Ionian', the name of a specific Greek clan that inhabited the eastern Mediterranean coast.

ALEXANDER, THE MACEDONIAN KING

Alexander (356–323 BCE) remains one of the world's legendary military commanders, famous for never being defeated in battle. This young ruler of the small kingdom of Macedon united Greece into one kingdom within a couple of years of ascending the throne at the age of twenty. After this, with his loyal army, he blazed through and conquered the enormous and powerful Persian Empire in just ten years. He soon took on the trappings of the Persian emperor. From starting out as part of a rather egalitarian Greek brotherhood, he began to insist on being addressed as 'Shahenshah' or 'King of Kings'. He started calling himself God and insisted that people prostrate themselves in front of him.

THE MACEDONIAN PHALANX

Alexander's men were trained to fight in tight Greek military formations called *phalanxes*, and each carried an extremely long spear, around 15 to 20 feet long, called a *sarissa*. This had been introduced by Alexander's father, King Philip. The battle formations became very difficult to defeat and, along with brilliant tactics and strategy, made Alexander's army practically invincible.

ALEXANDER AND BUCEPHALUS, BATTLE OF ISSUS MOSAIC

◆ SHASHIGUPTA, THE ALLY ◆

So, in 327 BCE, at the age of thirty, Alexander and his men arrived at India's doorstep. He was accompanied by an Indian mercenary leader called Sisycottus (possibly Shashigupta), who had been serving the Persian governor of Bactria before his defeat. Sisycottus attached himself to Alexander and was later made the governor of the mountain city of Aornos for his services.

Alexander invited all the chieftains of the former Persian satrapy of Gandhara to submit to him peacefully. Ambhi, the ruler of Takshashila, complied, but some hill tribes such as the Ashvakas and Ashvakayanas (in present-day north-eastern Afghanistan) refused to submit. Alexander defeated these tribes in battle. Soon, all the Indian kingdoms under Persian rule came under Alexander's control.

However, Alexander was a man of unlimited ambition and wanted to conquer further east.

◀ PORUS, THE VALIANT OPPONENT ▶

Alexander now had to face an independent ruler, Porus (King Puru), who reigned over the land of Pauravas, which lay in the part of Punjab now in Pakistan, between the rivers Jhelum (Hydaspes) and Chenab. Porus was a strong and brave leader who put up a fierce fight by all accounts but his armies were overpowered by Alexander's, according to Greek accounts. The ancient Greek historian Plutarch describes Porus as a giant of a man at six feet nine inches. He says that when seated on an elephant, Porus, being so large, appeared to be a horseman mounted on his horse!

Porus famously demanded that Alexander treat him like a king, even though he was a captive. Alexander was so impressed with Porus's bravery in battle, his regal persona and his courage that he reinstated Porus as king to rule under his name and even helped him conquer some nearby territories.

◀ ALEXANDRIAS SPROUT EVERYWHERE ▶

Alexander's favourite horse, Bucephalus, who had been presented to him by his father when he was thirteen, died during his battle with Porus on the banks of the Jhelum. Alexander did rather enjoy naming cities – new and conquered – after himself. An occasional thought was spared for various favourite pets that had died in his service. In fact, there is an ancient city somewhere in India, named after Alexander's deceased dog, Peritas, who saved Alexander's life during the siege of present-day Multan.

ALEXANDER'S CONQUESTS AND A FEW ALEXANDRIAS

There were up to 70 distinct Alexandrias across Alexander's empire, of which the most famous is the Alexandria in Egypt, which has retained its name to this day. In ancient times, it was renowned for its lighthouse, the Pharos – one of the Seven Wonders of the Ancient World – and its world-renowned library. Nine of the Alexandrias were founded in South Asia, across Afghanistan and India.

Alexander settled a mixture of Greeks and Persians in the thousands alongside the natives in each new city in South Asia. Many continue to flourish under new names. Of these, the one which remains most well-known today is Alexandria Arachosia, known as Kandahar today. The name is a corruption of Alexandria which became Iskanderiya that went on to become Kandahar!

◆ ALEXANDER'S MEN REFUSE TO GO ON ◆

After the battle with Porus, Alexander was now at the banks of the River Beas (the Greeks called it the Hyphasis) near what is now Amritsar in Punjab.

It was a common Greek belief that the world was flat and ended after India. Alexander wanted to continue pressing eastward because he *really* wanted to see the edge of the world!

However, this time he had a far more formidable foe to face. Across the Beas began the vast territory of the Nandas, extending from Bengal to Punjab. Alexander's men had had a hard time even overcoming Porus, whose kingdom was much smaller than the mighty Nanda Empire.

When the soldiers heard that they would have to face an army many, many times larger than Porus's, they flatly refused to march on. They were tired in mind and body, and wanted to enjoy their war loot in peace back home with their families. Alexander had no choice but to accept their decision. He had to turn back, even though he thought the world's edge was just a few kilometres to the east. Let's just say that he would have been in for a shock had he carried forth and stumbled upon the rest of Asia!

◀● ALEXANDER GOES BACK ●▶

On his way back home, Alexander decided to take a different route from the one he had taken to come to India. He and part of his army travelled down the River Indus and started on what turned out to be a death march through the arid deserts of Gedrosia (now Gwadar in Pakistan). Most of his army perished on the way back to Babylon. Within two years, Alexander himself was dead at the young age of thirty-two in Babylon (Iraq) due to illness, while his vast empire was divided up among his generals. They fought each other for decades. Finally, Asia came under the control of his general, Seleucus Nicator.

It is interesting to note that while Alexander's conquest of a part of India was tremendously important to the ancient Greeks as a symbol of Greece conquering the world, nowhere in Indian texts do we find any mention of Alexander or his supposedly earth-shattering conquest. Perhaps for most ancient Indians, it was more like an annoying border skirmish than an outright invasion.

◀● ARISTOTLE AND CALLISTHENES ●▶

Aristotle is one of the most famous Greek philosophers of all time. King Phillip of Macedon had invited him to tutor Alexander.

Aristotle wrote books on a wide variety of topics. His nephew Callisthenes accompanied Alexander on his conquests. We don't know whether Alexander sent an elephant to Aristotle, but he may have as Aristotle wrote an accurate description of an elephant he seems to have seen. Alexander did patronize philosophers, and we know that Callisthenes had sent astronomical data to Aristotle from Babylon.

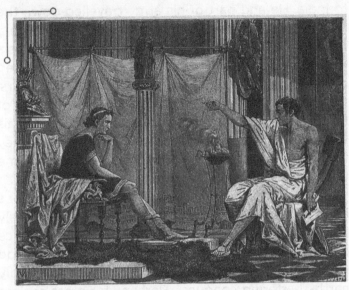

YOUNG ALEXANDER (LEFT) AND HIS TUTOR ARISTOTLE

THE RISE OF CHANDRAGUPTA MAURYA

Chandragupta Maurya (reign: 321–298 BCE) founded the Mauryan Empire, the first ever pan-Indian empire. It was also the largest empire ever in India, spanning more area than even the British as it also included regions of present-day Afghanistan and Central Asia. Chandragupta was a student at Takshashila under Acharya Chanakya, who was his mentor and guide throughout his life. In 321 BCE, just five years after

Alexander left India, he defeated the mighty Nandas and was crowned emperor of the Mauryan Empire.

Chandragupta's origins are cloaked in mystery, and most of what we know of him is from Buddhist and Jain legends. He is also mentioned in some Greek texts, who referred to him as 'Sandrocottus' and mentioned that he used to visit the Greek camp in Takshashila.

He was probably of warrior origin, perhaps from the Moriya Kshatriya clan, though some think he belonged to a poor family and was apprenticed to a hunter. Legend has it that Chandragupta was somewhat of an animal whisperer. There are many fanciful tales about Chandragupta recounted by the Roman writer Justin – from the time a wild elephant came and bowed to him, offering to carry him to war, to when a wild lion came and licked him as he slept!

While Chandragupta was working with the hunter in a small village, a legend goes that he met a learned professor of political science who was passing by, a Brahmin named Chanakya, who had been greatly insulted in the Nanda court. Chanakya saw promise in Chandragupta, adopted him as his protégé and took him to Takshashila. Together, their ambitious goal was to overthrow the Nanda dynasty once Chandragupta completed his studies.

◆ CHANDRAGUPTA VERSUS THE NANDAS ◆

At first, Chandragupta and Chanakya tried to displace King Dhanananda from his power base at Pataliputra (now Patna). Their attempt, however, was crushed, and they had to flee for their lives. They made their way back to Takshashila and hid from the emperor's men as they planned their next move. Eventually, they decided to first conquer the outer regions of the Nanda empire.

They entered a military alliance with King Parvatak, a ruler at the periphery of the Nanda Empire. Together, they subjugated the Punjab region. Chandragupta gradually made his way eastward, conquering one territory after the other until he defeated the last Nanda king.

The last battle was fierce, and an important Buddhist text, *Milindpanho*, gives absurd-sounding (and very likely exaggerated) figures for the losses. It claims that 1,000,000,000 soldiers died, 10,000 elephants perished, 100,000 horses were killed in this clash and so on.

There is also a legend that says that Parvatak's son Malayaketu, with whom Chandragupta was to share the throne, was conveniently crushed to death by a triumphal arch that fell on him during the victory procession. This gave rise to rumours of sabotage.

Chandragupta was now the ruler of a vast empire. The backbone of his empire was its army. Greek sources tell us that the Mauryans may have had the largest army in the world at the time, with 600,000 foot soldiers, 30,000 cavalrymen, 9,000 war elephants and 8,000 chariots.

◆ CHANDRAGUPTA VERSUS SELEUCUS ◆

The western borders of the Mauryan Empire overlapped with Seleucus Nicator's kingdom. Seleucus was one of Alexander's generals who had taken over his Asian territories after his leader's death. Seleucus dreamt of an empire grander than Alexander's and kept trying to invade Chandragupta's territories, including parts that had previously belonged to the Greeks.

In 305 BCE, Seleucus was defeated by Chandragupta and had to sign what must have been a humiliating treaty, whereby he gave present-day Afghanistan, some of Central Asia and possibly his daughter in marriage to Chandragupta. In return for all this, he received only 500 elephants! Seleucus, however, made the best of it and put his

SELEUCUS NICATOR

hard-earned elephants to good use in the battle with his neighbouring king Antigonus on the other side of his kingdom in what is now Syria.

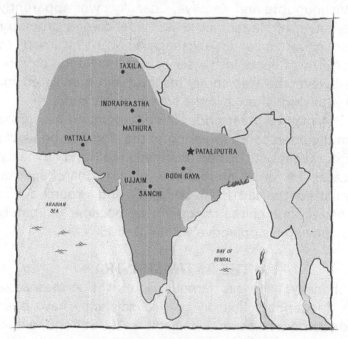

CHANDRAGUPTA MAURYA'S EMPIRE

Jain sources say that Chandragupta became a disciple of the Jain saint Bhadrabahu and took *sanyasa*. He went to Karnataka in 297 BCE with the saint. A legend says that he starved himself to death in a cave in Chandragiri Mountain in Shravanabelagola, now in Karnataka.

CHANAKYA, THE STRATEGIST

The mysterious kingmaker Chanakya was the force that propelled Chandragupta to the height of power and fame. Also known by other names such as Vishnugupta and Kautilya, Chanakya was apparently a native of Magadha. He was a renowned professor of governance in Takshashila, who returned to offer his talents in the service of the Nanda empire. However, he was sorely insulted and humiliated for his unsightly looks in the Nanda king's court.

A man of great pride, Chanakya untied his *shikha* in the open court, swearing to the king that he would not retie it until he had destroyed the Nanda dynasty. Later he encountered the young Chandragupta, plucked the lad from obscurity and groomed him into the matchless conqueror he became, ultimately achieving his objective within 10 to 15 years.

◆ THE *ARTHASHASTRA* ◆

Chanakya and his famous book, the *Arthashastra* - a legendary text on political science - have been described in several ancient texts. Still, no actual copy existed for modern Indians to study - that is, until 1905 when a priest living near Tanjore (now Thanjavur) in Tamil Nadu went to the chief librarian of the government library and handed over a Sanskrit manuscript. He claimed that it had been in his family for many generations. When research was done, it was discovered that this was the only existing copy of the *Arthashastra*.

The *Arthashastra* deals with kings – how they can gain, keep and even regain power, and their duties towards their subjects. The messages it advocates are extreme watchfulness, extensive pre-planning and ultimate control.

Although the author promotes the use of fair and, if required, foul means to attain his goals, he also links the duty and authority of a ruler very closely to his subjects' welfare. In his mind, the ideal king (and state) is like a stern, wise, all-knowing but compassionate father. The ruler is responsible for maintaining peace and order, looking after the weak and vulnerable, appropriately punishing the guilty, all the while ensuring that his hold on power doesn't slip away. It also has maxims for the common people. The *Arthashastra* mentions that truthfulness, uprightness, not injuring others, freedom from malice, compassion and forbearance are duties common to all. From how to trick your rivals to gain power to the use of spies and poison and everything in between, the *Arthashastra* makes for interesting (and often amusing) reading.

◆ CHANAKYA'S SAYINGS ◆

Chanakya is also known for his maxims, gathered together in Chanakya Niti (or 'Chanakya's policies'). We have used some of them in the book.

◉ *'Do not expose to others what you have planned in your mind. Work on it, keeping it as secret, as an incantation.'*

◉ *'It is by listening that a man learns about dharma. It is by listening that he gets rid of bad thoughts. It is by listening that he gathers knowledge. It is by listening that he achieves salvation.'* (Here, listening is the equivalent of reading)

◉ *'We should do every task, small or big, to the best of our ability. This is something we can learn from lions.'*

◉ *'Do not be too straightforward. Straight trees are cut down, while crooked trees are left standing.'*

WHAT THE GREEKS SAW

The India that Alexander and his men rode into would have looked significantly different from what we see today. Alexander brought historians and writers with him who recorded what they saw in detail. On his way back, Alexander sent one part of his army with his general Nearchus, who sailed along the coast to Iran. Nearchus's accounts, titled *Indica*, have not survived but have been quoted in later Greek texts, with his observations of India's people, rivers, animals, armies and customs.

◀● GREEN BY NATURE ●▶

India was simply filled with dense forests in ancient times – it was one big subcontinental forest! The Greeks describe this abundance of greenery.

Quintus Curtius Rufus, a later Roman historian who collated the Greek accounts of India in his book titled *The Histories of Alexander the Great*, quotes the Greeks as saying that across the River Jhelum 'the forests extended over an almost boundless tract of country, and abounded with stately trees that rose to an extraordinary height [...] the climate is tolerable, for the dense shade mitigates the violence of the heat, and copious springs supply the land with an abundance of water.'

The accounts also mention trees that rose to 100 feet and took four men to clasp them around. For the lands across the River Ravi, the Greeks remarked, 'the banks were covered with a dense forest [...] filled with wild peacocks.' If we visit these regions today, the only abundance we see is of flat, very flat agricultural land, rolling on endlessly as far as the eye can view!

◆ TAKSHSHILA, A TOP-TEN UNIVERSITY ◆

The Indian regions of the Persian Empire were divided into two, accounting for two of the empire's twenty-three provinces or satrapies. They were: the seventh satrapy called Gadara, which comprised northern parts of present-day Pakistan (the kingdoms of Gandhara and Kamboja), and the twentieth satrapy called Hindus, which consisted of most of modern Punjab, and Sindh in Pakistan.

As the Persians were generally tolerant of existing customs in their lands, local cultures were allowed to thrive, including the university of Takshashila, which was known to be *the* place to get a higher education in Asia, much like Harvard or Oxford universities today.

TAKSHASHILA'S RUINS, A UNESCO WORLD HERITAGE SITE

Takshashila was the capital of Gandhara. It was not a university in the modern sense as there was no central board that supervised what was taught, and no degrees were granted. Instead, it followed the ancient Indian *gurukul* system of education. The teachers were acknowledged throughout India to be an expert in their fields, and many different subjects were taught, such as the Vedas, law, medicine, military science and so on.

Each teacher was a college unto himself, and his students – the male ones – would generally live with him in his house. He decided how many and which students to teach, and what knowledge he would impart. There was no concept of advancing from one class to the next, and the studies would be complete if and when the teacher was satisfied.

The students would help their acharya or guru with the daily chores and collect alms in the city. They would sleep on the ground. Students who started sleeping on beds before completing their education were derisively called *khatavaruddha* – those 'tied to the bed'.

Many travellers have commented on how commonly khichri was eaten in India.

Though it was not common, there were women students in Takshashila who could learn philosophy and train in martial arts and the use of arms. Some women were professors as well.

Many famous people over the centuries studied in Takshashila, like Panini, the father of Sanskrit grammar, and Jivaka, the famous physician who gifted the Buddha an orchard.

Takshashila was finally destroyed in the Hunnic invasions of the fifth century CE, after a thousand years of pre-eminence.

◆ A LAND OF MANY LANGUAGES ◆

There were already several different languages spoken across the Indian subcontinent by the time of Alexander's invasion. Sanskrit was still the stronghold of the Brahmin elite, and was used for Vedic rites and rituals.

Most academic texts were composed in Sanskrit. However, the common people spoke different regional languages that had evolved over the centuries. These were called the Prakrit (meaning 'natural') languages. Yes, Prakrit was not just one language; it was a family of a range of dialects in different parts of India that grew apart over time, eventually giving us the modern regional languages we know today.

In Mauryan times, the Prakrit language in wide use was Ardhamagadhi, which was spoken in eastern India and would later evolve into the modern eastern Indian languages, including Bengali, Odia, Assamese and Bhojpuri.

Another Prakrit language was Shauraseni, spoken in the northern and western parts of the subcontinent, which gave rise to all the varieties of Hindi – Braj, Haryanvi, Khari Boli, Awadhi – as well as Punjabi, Gujarati, Rajasthani and Nepali.

Maharashtri was another kind of Prakrit spoken in ancient times and is the ancestor of the west Indian languages such as Marathi, Konkani and Sri Lankan Sinhalese.

◆ WORLD'S OLDEST NOSE JOB ◆

Did you know that plastic surgery was first developed in ancient India, more than 2,000 years ago? Despite the lack of modern anaesthesia, modern drugs and tools that we consider the minimum requirement for surgery, ancient doctors did surgeries like rhinoplasty (commonly known today as a 'nose job'), ear lobe reconstruction, cataract surgery, cleft lips and even delivery of babies by caesarean section!

Sushruta, an ancient surgeon who lived perhaps in the sixth century BCE in Varanasi, composed a long and comprehensive Sanskrit text called the *Sushruta Samhita*, which details different complex surgical procedures.

The nose-surgery procedure was used in India right until the 18th century when British surgeons saw some Indian doctors performing it on someone who had lost his nose in a battle, and carried the knowledge

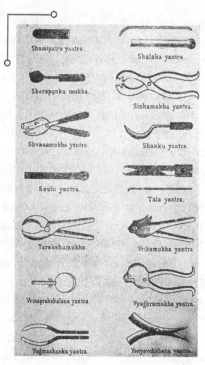

A FEW SURGICAL TOOLS FROM THE *SUSHRUTA SAMHITA*

back to London and Paris, starting a procedure that was long known as the 'Indian Nose'.

◆ CHARAKA, THE GO-TO HEALTH EXPERT ◆

Another significant person associated with Takshashila was the physician Charaka, credited with the *Charaka Samhita*, an important ancient medical treatise on the human body, its health, and disease prevention and cure. While we don't know if Charaka referred to a single person or a school of doctors, we can say that the *Charaka Samhita* is one of three great classics of Ayurveda.

Ayurveda is regarded as the oldest healthcare system in the world, and modern Ayurvedic doctors still use the *Charaka Samhita* for their medical training. Imagine, an ancient book still relevant to us after thousands of years and even after the advent of modern medicine! Not only that, Ayurveda is becoming increasingly popular in the West, where it is being offered as alternative medicine.

The *Charaka Samhita* has startlingly modern views for its time. It claims that health and disease are not predetermined, and life can be prolonged by human effort and lifestyle. It also states that all areas of life impact one's health and lays as much emphasis on the preventive aspects of health such as nutrition, exercise and meditation, as it does on curing diseases.

Indians are quite familiar with many of the remedies prescribed by Ayurveda, though we are not usually aware that these concoctions were thought up 2,500 years ago. Remedies such as Chyawanprash, a daily tonic for general health, still lovingly spooned into the mouths of Indian children by their doting grandmas, was first prescribed in the *Charaka Samhita*!

Charaka's work was translated into early Persian and Arabic by writers on medicine and taken to the West, where it influenced medical science.

◆ DANDAMIS ◆

There are many tales of Alexander's encounters with Indian philosophers. Alexander met some gymnosophists or 'naked philosophers' – probably followers of Jainism. He was impressed by their powers of endurance and asked them to go back with him. However, their aged leader Dandamis forbade his disciples to do this.

Dandamis was immune to Alexander's threats and bribes. He is supposed to have given a speech as described in the story, though to Alexander himself (not his nephew). Dandamis's words convinced Alexander that he was indeed a free man, so Alexander made no attempt to compel him.

❖ Y FOR YOGA ❖

Yoga is a vast collection of spiritual, mental and physical exercises from ancient India. Today the term is normally used for Hatha Yoga, an exercise using asanas. The word can mean joining or concentration, as explained in Patanjali's *Yoga Sutras* – probably the most important book on yoga, written in the second century CE.

Based on some of the postures depicted on Indus Valley seals, it is speculated that yoga was practised in the Harappan civilization.

❖ FASCINATING FASHION ❖

Nearchus described the very unusual fashion tastes of the people of Takshashila. Well-born Indian men wore whiter-than-white robes, dyed their beards in all colours, sported multicoloured, high-heeled platform sandals and carried umbrellas to shield themselves from the sun!

Nearchus also spoke of an Indian region with a most unusual custom, where kingship was not based on dynasty nor ability, but on appearances – the most handsome man in the kingdom was crowned King. Some think this refers to a king named Sophites (perhaps King Saubhuti).

When Alexander reached King Sophites's capital with his men, the king appeared before them. Historian Quintus Curtius Rufus mentions that 'he (King Sophites) was distinguished above all the other barbarians by his tall and handsome figure' and wore extremely rich clothes, golden sandals and a profusion of pearls on his body. It is also interesting to note that the handsome king Sophites, apparently, surrendered without as much as a squeak to Alexander.

Nearchus also describes the royal procession of King Sophites as detailed in the story.

HAIL THE ELEPHANTS

Indians were the earliest to tame elephants. Asiatic elephants are smaller than their African cousins (which have never been tamed) and have been used for transport, construction and war in India and South-East Asia since ancient times. The earliest mention of

COIN OF THE MAURYA EMPIRE, WITH AN ELEPHANT SYMBOL

captive elephants is on Harappan seals from 5,000 years ago.

Indian elephants often have small pink marks or dots spotting their ears, faces and trunks. They have a close bond with their trainers, known as *mahavats* or mahouts. Since elephants and humans have about the same life expectancy, these relationships are often lifelong. They often show affection by wrapping their trunks around their human friends.

Indian elephants are known to be very social and intelligent. Young elephants are very playful and adventurous. They have been trained to play sports like cricket and football.

The elephant dance in the book was personally observed and described by the Roman historian Arrian, though much later than Alexander's time.

Acknowledgements

Vedita, Vihana and Soham, thank you for all your ideas and brainstorming on this series in our many lockdown sessions!

Thank you also to our other nieces and nephew, Pia, Neil and Uma, for providing us valuable insights into the behaviour of the young of the species...our readers.

We are thankful to our friends and family for their forbearance with our foibles and idiosyncrasies over the years – and yet providing us their unstinting support.

A big thank you to Priya Kuriyan for her delightful illustrations.

We are, as always, indebted to our fabulous editor Vatsala, who indulges us.

• • • • • • • • • • • • • •

LOOK OUT FOR THEIR NEXT ADVENTURE!
Akbar and the Agents from the East

It's the Mughal court, and the centre of drama, intrigue, action...and dangers! When Zoya, Noor, Rohan, Ansh and Elfu land right in the middle of Akbar's reign, there's no saying what lies in store for them... and whether they can handle the perils they have to face in another time, another place!